D0199463

24944

# The Fate
# – of the –
# Yellow Woodbee

N5156H

Library
Oakland S.U.M.

# Trailblazer Books

## Also by Dave and Neta Jackson

*Hero Tales: A Family Treasury of True Stories
From the Lives of Christian Heroes* (Volumes I, II, & III)

# The Fate
## – of the –
# Yellow Woodbee

**Dave & Neta Jackson**

Story illustrations by
Julian Jackson

## BETHANY HOUSE PUBLISHERS
MINNEAPOLIS, MINNESOTA 55438

*The Fate of the Yellow Woodbee*
Copyright © 1997
Dave and Neta Jackson

Illustrations © 1997
Bethany House Publishers

Story illustrations by Julian Jackson.
Cover design and illustration by Catherine Reishus McLaughlin.

Scripture quotations are from the King James Version of the Bible.

All rights reserved. No part of this publication may be reproduced, stored in a retrieval system, or transmitted in any form or by any means—electronic, mechanical, photocopying, recording, or otherwise—without the prior written permission of the publisher and copyright owners.

Published by Bethany House Publishers
A Ministry of Bethany Fellowship International
11400 Hampshire Avenue South
Minneapolis, Minnesota 55438
www.bethanyhouse.com

Printed in the United States of America by
Bethany Press International, Minneapolis, Minnesota 55438

**Library of Congress Cataloging-in-Publication Data**

Jackson, Dave
    The fate of the yellow woodbee / Dave and Neta Jackson.
       p.    cm. — (Trailblazer books)
    Summary: A fictionalized account of the five missionaries who carried God's word to the fierce Aucas, or Huaorani, of Ecuador in 1956.
    ISBN 1–55661–743–7 (pbk.)
    1. Huao Indians—Juvenile Fiction.
[1. Huao Indians—Fiction. 2. Indians of South America—Ecuador—Fiction. 3. Missionaries—Fiction. 4. Ecuador—Fiction. 5. Christian life—Fiction.]
    I. Jackson, Neta. II. Title. III. Series: Jackson, Dave. Trailblazer books.
PZ7.J132418Fat    1997
[Fic]—dc21
                                        97–21064
                                            CIP
                                            AC

It should be noted that the correct name for the Indian people featured in this book is *Waorani*, the name they call themselves. However, we have used the name *Auca* because it was the name by which they were known to outsiders at the time of the story, and it seemed confusing to switch back and forth between chapters.

While Niwa, Dabu, and Moipa are authentic Auca names, their characters in this book are fictional. Everyone else, and the events that happened to them, are real. The pet parrot was actually donated by Mincaye.

To reduce complexity, some liberty has been taken in terms of where the missionaries were stationed when planning and carrying out Operation Auca. In this book, most flights are said to have originated from the Shell Mera base. In reality, the final flights were made out of the closer base of Arajuno.

Some of the Auca dialog may sound backward to English-speaking people. It is merely an attempt to give some flavor of the Auca sentence structure.

DAVE AND NETA JACKSON are a husband/wife writing team who have authored and coauthored many books on marriage and family, the church, and relationships, including the books accompanying the Secret Adventures video series, the Pet Parables series, the Caring Parent series, and the newly released *Hero Tales*, volumes I and II.

The Jacksons have two married children: Julian, the illustrator for TRAILBLAZER BOOKS, and Rachel, who has recently blessed them with a granddaughter, Havah Noelle. Dave and Neta make their home in Evanston, Illinois, where they are active members of Reba Place Church.

# CONTENTS

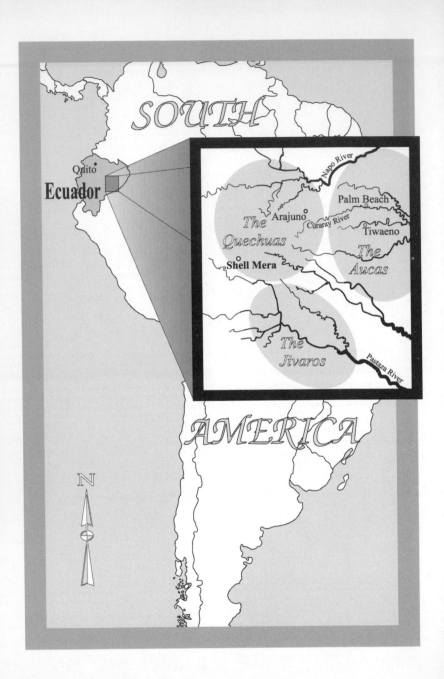

# Chapter 1

# Saved by the "Woodbee"

THE SUDDEN SILENCE made Niwa look up into the tall balsa trees. The brightly colored parrots had stopped squawking at each other. The howler monkeys weren't screeching. "Shh!" he whispered to Dabu and Moipa and the other two boys from his village who had come on the fishing expedition. "Someone's coming."

In the middle of the shallow river, the young boys stood as still as the shafts of golden sunlight stabbing down through the green jungle canopy overhead. Their fishing spears remained at the ready. Each boy's dark eyes searched the too-silent jungle . . . all, that is, except

Moipa. His eyes caught the shadow of an armored catfish lazily snaking its way across the sandy bottom of the river, whipping its powerful tail in easy strokes.

Moipa couldn't resist. With all his might he flung his spear at the fish. *"Baru!"* he yelled. "I got it!" He splashed forward through the water.

Before he had taken three steps, two men jumped off the high mudbank along the other shore and began running toward the boys. They held their nine-foot-long spears at the ready, but not for spearing fish.

"Run!" yelled Niwa. "Killers from downriver. They'll spear us for sure!"

White spray flew as bare, brown feet pounded through the shallow water. With strong, agile legs Niwa leaped onto an old log that angled down into the river and raced up it into the jungle. Just before he ducked into a stand of tall bamboo, he heard Moipa's voice screaming in pain. He looked back but could not see his friend anywhere. Niwa started to return to help Moipa when he saw one of the other boys go down into the river with a spear through his leg. An enemy from downriver ran toward the boy, ready to launch another spear as he yelled, *"Baru! Baru!"*

There was nothing Niwa could do. He turned and fled into the bamboo. He didn't dare go back. He couldn't have helped if he had. All the Aucas from his village of Tiwaeno lived in fear of the "Downrivers." If he went back, they would surely kill him, too.

Niwa ran and ran through the jungle as nettles stung his bare skin and sticks scratched his legs. He scrambled up the steep hillside to get away from the Curaray River as fast as possible. The boys had come a long way from home that morning on their fishing trip. There was always a risk of an attack from the Downrivers, the neighboring tribe of Aucas with whom Niwa's people constantly feuded. But there hadn't been any killing for several months, so the Aucas in his village had become lax in their caution. And the boys had gone far from their home along the Tiwaeno.

At the top of the ridge, Niwa ran west down a narrow mud trail along the mountains that separated the Curaray River from the Tiwaeno River. The pounding of his heart in his chest kept time with the pounding of his feet on the jungle floor. His breathing sounded like the swish of wind in the trees during a heavy storm, but he couldn't stop. The Downrivers might be right behind him.

Once, his eyes caught sight of jaguar tracks in the soft mud along his trail. Niwa stopped and looked around, trying to silence his heavy breathing. Niwa was not someone who was scared easily. He realized that the tracks had been coming toward him. So unless the great cat circled around, it was already behind him, heading the other way. *Maybe it will get the Downrivers,* he thought. In any case, he couldn't wait. There might be danger ahead of him, but there was certain death behind him from the Downrivers. He had to get away and warn his village. He continued his jog-run, turning south off the ridge until he came to a familiar hunting trail.

He was not far from the Tiwaeno River now. He wound his way down the mountain and splashed through the clear-running stream along which his own village was located. Finally, so exhausted that he couldn't run another step, he climbed up the bank to the clearing surrounding his village of Tiwaeno.

"Help! The Downrivers attacked us," he gasped. "In our waiting, they may be coming here."

"If they are following you," snapped a toothless old woman sipping a sticky plantain drink from a gourd, "why did you come back here? You will just lead them to us." She spat into the smoldering fire in front of her.

"Yes," chimed in some other women. "Go away! We don't want you here. Go back to the jungle!"

Niwa ignored them as he searched several of the communal houses, each one sheltering four or five families and their cooking fires, looking for the men of the village. Surely they would get ready to fight. But the houses and the hammocks were empty. "The men have gone hunting!" piped up one of the younger children. "Feeling sick, only Gikita stays in his hammock."

Niwa hurried to Gikita's house. Like all the other houses in the village, it was nothing more than a roof of palm leaves without walls. Even though Gikita was only forty years old, he was the oldest man in the village. Auca men died young from all the killing that happened between villages, but also within each village. Niwa found Gikita in his hammock. The man's eyes were closed, and he looked awful.

"Gikita, Gikita! The Downrivers attacked us while we were fishing in the river. You must come and help."

Gikita rolled his eyes and murmured, "Our river? The Tiwaeno?"

"No, not the Tiwaeno, the Curaray, the big river

across the hill."

"Then leave me alone," moaned Gikita. "I'm much too sick to do anything today. Don't bother me. Maybe tomorrow if I am better we will go kill some Downrivers."

Niwa left Gikita's side and went looking for someone from his family. Nampa, his older brother, was out hunting with the men. And his sister Gimari— she might be anywhere. But his mother was probably upriver making clay pots. She was always making new pots. He set out to find her. As he passed the other houses, the women again yelled at him. "Go back into the jungle. You will bring the Downrivers to us."

"If the men were here," one yelled, "they would spear you for coming back to the village. Get out!" She picked a smoldering stick from her cooking fire and began chasing Niwa with it. Even his Aunt Mintaka joined in the chase, waving a sharp machete high above her head.

Just then Niwa saw his mother coming down the trail from the clay bank. Like the other adults of the village, Akawo's ears were pierced with large wooden plugs, her only ornament. Over her shoulder she carried a woven sack with clay pots in it. "Mother!" he yelled.

"Niwa, what is it?" she called in alarm as she saw him being chased. "Run faster, Niwa. Run faster!" And she began running toward him.

The manioc plants in the village garden caught at his ankles as he ran through them. He felt childish running to his mother for safety. At eleven years old, he shouldn't need her to protect him. He should be protecting her.

"What are you doing?" his mother challenged the two women who came to a stop in the middle of the manioc patch some fifteen feet away.

"Tell that boy of yours to go into the jungle and not to come back here while those Downrivers are after him," the woman with the smoldering stick said. Then she heaved it halfheartedly in their direction.

"But don't you care about Dabu and Moipa and the others?" Niwa cried. He stood partially behind his mother, bending over with his hands on his knees as he tried to catch his breath.

"At least they weren't foolish enough to come straight back to the village," his Aunt Mintaka said.

"Yes, but I think Moipa got speared," said Niwa. "I heard him screaming. He might be dead. They all might be dead!"

"Tomorrow, then, we may be going downriver to kill some enemies," said his aunt, "—if the men aren't hunting," she added as an afterthought. "But for now, you get out of here." Mintaka started forward again, raising the machete as she picked her way through the plants.

Just then Niwa heard a loud buzzing sound in the sky. He looked up and saw what looked like a large yellow bird.

His aunt stopped her threatening advance and looked up as well. "It's a woodbee," she said as a look of horror spread over her face. "A woodbee, with *cowodi* inside!"

Both women turned and ran back to the village shouting, "Woodbee, woodbee!" as they pointed to the sky. Even Niwa's mother followed them without a glance back at Niwa.

Niwa watched the noisy yellow bird for a few moments and then went over to the tall stump of a balsa tree that still stood in the middle of the manioc patch. It was taller than any of the men in the village. They had left it in the middle of the garden because it was too much trouble to dig it out. Niwa climbed up on top of it to be closer to the woodbee. The women might be afraid, but it seemed to him that this strange yellow bird had just saved him from their anger. He wanted to get a better look at it.

From the top of the stump he could see that back in the village the women and children had panicked. They called to one another, "Woodbee! It's a woodbee!" While some stood staring, others ran for the cover of their houses.

Niwa had often seen small insects called woodbees buzzing through the upper branches of the jungle trees, but they had not been bright yellow, and they certainly did not look like this giant one. He remembered the stories the adults told of the giant woodbees. They were said to be as large as a small house, and they supposedly carried *cowodi* in their bellies. *Cowodi*—were there really such creatures as white men? Niwa found it hard to believe, and certainly if they existed, they wouldn't be cannibals.

Why, if white men ate people, that would make them more savage than the Downrivers. Yet, it seemed to Niwa, this woodbee had saved him from his aunt's machete. He looked hard at the strange bird to see if he could spot any of the *cowodi* in its belly.

The woodbee was circling. He could tell it was very large by the slow way it turned. He had never heard such a noisy bird. It couldn't really be an insect, a "bee." It had to be some kind of a bird.

Even while Niwa watched, the woodbee stopped circling and flew off over the trees.

Crossing his legs, Niwa sat down on the top of the stump and put his chin in his hands while he looked at the village. The sun was hot on his golden-brown skin. Soon he saw the women and children who had been scared by the woodbee coming out of their houses, and everyone was talking together. He thought that with all the excitement over the woodbee, no one would notice him if he sneaked back. He would probably be safe.

But the thought of the women of the village chasing him caused him to frown. It wasn't fair. There was so much killing and violence among his people. If a man became angry with his wife, he might spear her. If an argument broke out between two people, one might kill the other while he or she slept. Even children weren't safe. It was a life of terror that made Niwa sometimes feel like running away. But . . . where would he go? To whom could he turn? Weren't there any villages that lived in peace with each other?

## Chapter 2

# Operation Auca

NATE SAINT TAPPED THE FUEL GAGE for the gas tank in the right wing of the yellow single-engine airplane. The missionary pilot already knew the left tank was empty. The gage did not change. "Not much left," he said, readjusting his baseball cap on his blond, close-cropped hair and looking out over the jungle below.

He'd developed the habit of talking out loud even when he flew alone. It was a way of keeping himself company. Even if there had been passengers in the backseat, he would have had to shout over the noise of the engine to make himself heard.

The young pilot nudged the control stick to the left and then to the right, making a gentle S turn to study the ground below him better. Still there was no sign of the Jivaro village where fellow missionary Roger Youderian was stranded waiting for medical supplies.

Nate was looking for a jungle village with a new airstrip near it that Roger had encouraged the Indians to hack out of the jungle. Nate had flown over the village a few days earlier when the airstrip was almost finished and couldn't understand why he was having trouble finding it again. In the clear afternoon air, he could see for a hundred miles, but there were no breaks in the sea of green below him.

Finally, to his great relief, he saw a thin curl of smoke rising from the jungle near a brown streak in the green. *A river,* he thought, and beside it he began to make out a small clearing with thatched-roof houses. "Thank You, Lord," Nate said aloud. He put the bulky earphones over his head and picked up the microphone to call his wife. Marj Saint operated the missionary radio back at the mission base, Shell Mera.

He clicked the button twice and said, "This is fifty-six Henry—I'll be over Jimmy's place in two minutes." The license on the wings of the Piper Family Cruiser read N5156H, and "fifty-six Henry" stood for the last three characters of that number. "Jimmy's place" was a code to keep the oil companies that might be listening to their radio broadcasts from knowing where they were and what was happening.

The missionaries couldn't risk outsiders taking advantage of their contacts with these primitive tribes.

"Fifty-six Henry—I'll be over Jimmy's place in two minutes," Nate repeated. "Over."

The radio crackled to life in Nate's earphones. Then came the reassuring sound of his wife's voice. "Roger, fifty-six Henry. Roger and out."

With a sigh of relief, Nate pulled off his earphones and eased the throttle back, starting the plane's descent toward the riverside village. But when he got over it, there was no airstrip. As he circled, he could see that the houses were of a different design than the ones he was expecting. This was not a Jivaro Indian village or a Quechuan Indian village. And it certainly was not the village where Roger waited for him.

He put his small yellow plane in a tight circle. If it was not Jivaro or Quechuan, then it had to be an Auca village.

Nate and the other missionaries with whom he worked in the jungles of Ecuador had often talked of trying to find the dreaded Aucas. They needed the Gospel as much as any other people, but no white person had made contact with them in their jungle setting and lived to tell about it. This had been true since the sixteenth-century conquistadors had been killed trying to cross their land. In 1667, Pedro Suarez, a Jesuit missionary, had been speared to death when he tried to set up a mission station in their territory. Then in the nineteenth century came gold prospectors and rubber hunters. They killed or enslaved Indians wherever they found them. But just as often, Aucas killed them. Now, in the twentieth century, several oil company explorers had been speared.

The surrounding Quechua Indians were terrified of the Aucas. In fact, the word Auca was a Quechuan word meaning "savages." Even the head-hunting Jivaros stayed out of the Auca's jungle.

Nate watched below him as several women and children ran for cover in their wall-less houses. But he could see one boy in the middle of a small cleared field who did not run. The boy climbed on top of a stump and watched as Nate flew above him. Nate opened the window on his left and reached out to wave, but the boy did not respond. *Yes, the Aucas do look as wild as the reports have said,* he thought.

The Piper's little engine sputtered and coughed, then resumed its steady roar. He shivered; it was probably just a little water in the fuel, but this was not a place to go down. Even if he survived a crash landing, he might be speared by the "welcoming" party. And yet he had found the Aucas—at least one of their villages. He closed the window and circled higher to get a fix on his location. He would return. He glanced again at the fuel gage. It was bouncing dangerously close to the empty line. He had to get out of there.

Nate Saint had three small children back at Shell Mera, and even though a jungle missionary pilot's life was never "safe," he didn't take needless risks. As he circled higher, he reminded himself that he

had responsibilities. People depended upon him, like his little Kathie, only seven, and the baby, Philip.

And then there was five-year-old Steve. Just that morning, Steve had waved to him as he took off. Steve, with his buzz-cut blond hair, had tilted his head to one side, squinting into the morning sun. He was always there to wave to his dad—heading out or coming home.

Off toward the horizon Nate noticed a black column of smoke. The pilot shook his head to clear his mind. That must be the village where Roger waited. Possibly he had heard the sound of Nate's plane and made a big bonfire with lots of smoke to help guide him in. No Indian would make that much smoke without a purpose.

Nate checked his compass and looked around for distant mountains to use as landmarks. Slowly, with a lurch in his heart, he began to realize where he was. "That can't be right," he said aloud. "It's just impossible." How could he have been that far off course? He was an excellent pilot who had flown over the jungle hundreds of times. What had happened?

In a few minutes, he was over the village where Roger waited. The airstrip looked rough, but he decided to try it. After all, Roger was counting on him. Down he came, dodging a tall tree at the beginning of the little strip, and then his wheels hit the ground.

"Hey, I'm glad to see you!" Roger grinned as the propeller died, and Nate climbed out of the yellow plane. The tall, gawky young man with the unruly thatch of dark hair clapped Nate on the shoulder.

"Not as glad as I am to see you," Nate said wryly. "I'm almost out of juice. You still have those cans of gas I left with you for your lantern?"

After unloading the much-needed medical supplies and helping Roger give penicillin shots to many in the village sick with a jungle fever, Nate carefully poured two gallons of gas into the plane's gas tank. Then the two missionaries took off down the rough runway and set a course for Shell Mera where Marj and Roger's wife, Barbara, waited.

That night as they sat around the dinner table, the two couples were joined by three other missionary couples from the area: Jim and Elisabeth Elliot, Ed and Marilou McCully, and Pete and Olive Fleming. Nate filled them all in about his strange flight that afternoon.

"When's the last time I got my directions confused?" he asked.

Everyone shrugged. They couldn't think of any time when Nate had been lost.

"Well, this afternoon when I went down to pick up Roger, I got lost."

"Lost?" Jim Elliot said. Jim's good looks and charming smile hid a serious young man. "What do you mean? You made it back."

"Yes," said Nate, pushing the brim of his baseball cap up on his head. "But not until I found what I was supposed to find!"

"What do you mean?" asked Jim's wife, Elisabeth, curiously, pausing with her fork in mid-air.

Nate described finding the Auca village. "I have this deep feeling that the Lord allowed me to drift off course precisely so we would find that Auca village."

"I told you guys," hooted Jim Elliot with enthusiasm, "one of these days we were going to spot those people, and from then on they'd be marked for Christ. I agree with you, Nate. I think the Lord wanted us to find them. The time has come to take the Gospel to them."

"If we don't get to them with the Gospel," said Elisabeth, "I'm afraid the oil companies will wipe them out. Those big corporations are losing patience. Every time they try to explore Auca territory, they are attacked. They won't put up with it much longer. They are already pressing the Ecuadorian government to go in and remove the Aucas, and you know what that means—most will be shot."

"Hey—there's something else I just now thought of," said Nate. "Did you hear about that Auca woman on Don Carlos's hacienda?"

Most of the missionaries around the table shook their heads.

"Well," continued Nate, "about eight years ago an Auca woman came out of the jungle and sought refuge on his hacienda. Apparently she was going to be killed for—well, who knows why."

"Whew!" put in Pete Fleming. "It seems that all the Aucas do is kill people—if not outsiders, then one another." He absently pulled off his rimless glasses and rubbed his eyes thoughtfully.

"All the more reason to reach them with the

Gospel," said Nate. "Besides, my sister Rachel has met the woman. Her name is Dayuma, and Rachel is learning a little of her language."

"Language! That's what we need," said Jim. "That'll be the key to a successful contact."

"Then there is no doubt," said Ed McCully, putting an arm around his pregnant wife, Marilou. "God is preparing us to reach the Aucas, but how? Sighting them from the air or talking to a refugee who hasn't lived with them for years is a long way from risking our necks with first contact on their territory."

"Maybe so," said Nate excitedly. "These are just the first steps. We need a plan—an 'Operation Auca.' "

"Operation Auca," grinned Pete, settling his glasses back on his nose. "Has a nice ring. But we better keep it secret. If our plans get out, either the Ecuadorian government will try to stop us or the oil companies will try to horn in and ruin the whole project."

# Chapter 3

## Strange Gifts

THE AUCA BOY SAT ON TOP of the stump in the middle of the manioc patch for a long time. The women in the village paid no attention to him after the woodbee flew away.

Niwa started wondering, *Did the woodbee come for some other purpose, or did it possibly come to rescue me? Maybe the* cowodi *aren't so bad after all.* He hoped that they did ride in the belly of the woodbee, and he hoped that someday soon the woodbee would return. He would watch for it.

Finally, he got down off of the stump and wandered back home. He fed a banana to his pet parrot. The bird bobbed its beautiful green head up and down and stepped from side to side on its perch. At least his parrot was not angry with him. Then Niwa found a piece of smoked monkey tail on the rack over the fire and started eating it. He hadn't had any food since early that morning.

Everywhere he turned, in every house, around every fire, the only talk was about the coming of the woodbee. What did it mean? Why had it come? Would there be trouble from the *cowodi*—the outsiders?

No one asked him about the attack on the boys who had been fishing on the Curaray River. No one seemed to care.

Late that afternoon, Dabu staggered into the village half carrying Moipa. Moipa had lost so much blood from a spear wound through the shoulder that he fainted every few steps. His mother helped him into his hammock, but instead of asking him about what had happened, all she wanted to do was tell him about the woodbee. Soon he slipped into unconsciousness, and she left him.

As soon as Niwa could get Dabu alone he asked, "What happened to the other boys? Did they escape?"

"I don't see them," Dabu said, clenching his teeth angrily. "I never saw them come back. Doing all we could, we came home. What's this talk about a woodbee? Isn't anyone going to avenge the attack on us?"

That evening when the men returned, it was the same thing. They carried a large tapir slung on a pole between two men, but instead of bragging over such an important hunting success and rejoicing that there would be meat for the next couple days, the conversation turned immediately to the strange woodbee.

By the time darkness filled the jungle, the last two remaining boys from the fishing trip had not yet arrived. Niwa and Moipa were convinced that they had been killed in the attack.

Gikita, still recovering from his stomach sickness, sat by the main village fire and said, "Not being safe here, I think we should leave Tiwaeno. If the *cowodi* have found us, they will soon come to kill us with their fire sticks. We must move."

"No," said others. "What can a woodbee do? We have seen them before."

"I do not believe white cannibals ride in its belly," declared Niwa's mother, Akawo.

"That's because you don't want to face the truth," snapped a younger woman named Umi. "Your Dayuma ran away to the *cowodi* years ago and was probably eaten the day she arrived. You are not believing it because she was your daughter. Face the truth!"

"Face the truth! Face the truth!" cawed Niwa's parrot from his perch.

"Be quiet, you horrid bird!" yelled Akawo. Then with a loud moan she continued to Umi, "Because Wepe was going to kill her, Dayuma ran away. And she was your cousin, too. You should care."

Umi shrugged. "What difference does it make?"

"I still think we should leave Tiwaeno," insisted Gikita.

"Face the truth! Face the truth!" cawed the parrot.

In a rage, Akawo turned and threw a clay pot at the bird. With a wild screech the bird leaped to the side and flew to Niwa, where it landed on his head. Niwa got up and left the fire. What difference did all this talk make? The killing would continue, but he did not think it would come from the woodbee.

Several days later, Niwa woke up early. The whole village was quiet. Not even the pet parrots and caged spider monkeys were making any noise. The boy swung out of his hammock, threaded his way past the hammocks of the four families that shared the large thatched-roof shelter, and wandered outside. A heavy mist hung over the whole jungle, blocking out the tops of the trees. Instead of rising and blowing away on the breeze, small tendrils of smoke still rose from some of the fires and drifted throughout the village like snakes slithering through grass.

It was a strange day made stranger by the recent events that had disrupted the life of the small community.

Niwa walked out to the garden and climbed up onto the stump where he had watched the woodbee. Something had to change. But as he sat there, he began to be aware of a strange sound. At first it was a distant droning that was hardly noticeable, but then he recognized it. It was the woodbee, far away and high in the sky.

Niwa looked up, searching for a break in the mist, until his neck ached. And then he began seeing patches of blue, thinly appearing here and there in the sky overhead. While he watched, the sound of the woodbee got louder. It increased from a distant hum to the more familiar buzzing.

It was coming! And Niwa was the only person up to see it.

But not for long. By the time Niwa caught the first glimpse of the yellow bird in the patches of blue between the mist clouds, other people were coming out of their houses in the village. They, too, were looking up and calling to one another. Soon the whole village was astir.

A small breeze had come up and was quickly driving away the last remaining clouds, and the woodbee could be clearly seen directly overhead.

This time it was clear to everyone that a man—in fact, two men—were inside the woodbee. The villagers began to scream, *"Cowodi, cowodi!* Run for your life!"* Everyone suddenly seemed ready to take Gikita's advice to flee, and some began grabbing their spears, blowguns and darts, baskets, and other valuables and heading for the jungle.

Then Niwa saw that the woodbee had stopped circling over the village and had begun to circle over the nearby river. He ran down to the river to be closer. To him, the woodbee was a friend. It had saved him from Mintaka's machete.

*31*

As he stood on the sandbar at the river's edge, a wonderful thing happened. A long vine came out of the bottom of the woodbee with something shiny attached to it. The woodbee circled lower and lower, and at the same time the vine got longer, and the shiny thing came lower and lower until it was almost within Niwa's grasp. And then it dropped onto the sandy beach at the water's edge.

Niwa ran to pick it up. It was a metal pot with brightly colored ribbons attached, and it was filled with buttons and other strange things. He hurried to take it to the village. "Seeing what the *cowodi* have brought us, we cannot leave now," he yelled. "Look at this!"

In a short time, the woodbee flew off over the trees, and the villagers returned to their houses. The younger children eagerly grabbed the ribbons from Niwa. They put the ribbons around their heads and arms. Niwa, however, kept the buttons for his parrot. Akawo claimed the shiny pot, saying she was certain that her Dayuma had sent it to her.

The other stuff inside the pot felt like coarse sand. It tasted strange, and his mother threw it away.

Many of the Aucas still thought moving was the best idea, but their curiosity delayed them. A few days later the woodbee came again. This time it lowered a machete to them on the end of the long vine. Again the vine swung over the strip of sandy beach by the river, but then the machete landed in the water. Niwa was waving at the *cowodi* from the

top of his stump in the manioc garden, but before he could scramble down to the river and retrieve the machete, Gikita—who had recovered completely from his sickness—waded in to pick it up.

A machete was indeed a valuable item among the Aucas. Machetes and other metal items were rare in the jungle, and the Aucas obtained them only by stealing them from other tribes like the Quechuas or the Jivaros, who often traded with the *cowodi* white cannibals.

As the woodbee circled above, the Aucas could hear the men inside yelling words at them, but the Aucas just looked at one another and shrugged. No one understood what they were saying.

## Chapter 4

# A Carved Message

**O**PERATION AUCA was in full swing by October 1955 as the missionaries sat on the living room floor of their mission station one evening and discussed their strategy.

"What we need to do is win the Aucas over with gifts," said Elisabeth Elliot. Several others nodded in agreement. "Probably their only experience with outsiders has been violent," she continued. "No wonder they are always ready to fight."

"We could drop gifts from the plane," suggested Ed McCully.

Nate Saint frowned. "I don't know if that's

such a good idea," he said. "I've been talking to my sister, Rachel, about that Auca woman she's getting to know. She said that when the oil company planes dropped gifts, the Aucas thought that spears they had thrown up into the air had wounded the planes and the gifts had fallen out of its belly. They didn't even consider them gifts. Apparently, they thought it was the result of their victory in battle against the big 'bird.' "

"No, not birds," corrected Nate's wife, Marj. "Rachel said the Aucas call airplanes 'bees.' "

"You're right," Nate agreed. "I think she said they call them 'woodbees' or something like that."

"Then somehow we need to *give* the gifts to them," said Ed, bringing them back to the problem. "We can't just drop them from the sky. And we need to do it every week or so. Sooner or later their hostility has got to dissolve if we prove that we are friendly."

"Yeah, but how?" said Pete Fleming. "How are we going to *give* them gifts? I'm sure not volunteering to hike in there—at least not until we have some reason to trust that they won't spear us."

"Well," Nate said with a sly smile, "I've been working on a system of lowering a line to people on the ground to deliver things."

"Sure," Jim Elliot grinned. "I can just see them trying to catch a bundle on the end of a line as it flies by at sixty-five or seventy miles an hour."

"Yeah," laughed Ed, "and what'll they do if they *do* catch it? It won't be like a football, you know. It'll keep going and either yank them off the ground or break the line."

"No, no," said Roger Youderian, "you don't understand. Nate's developed a great system. He's tried it with me a couple times. He flies in a very tight circle overhead, and the drop package hangs at the end of a long line hundreds of feet below. The wind kind of blows it back, but because Nate is circling so tightly, the package actually ends up in the middle of that circle, like it was at the bottom of a whirlpool. By gradually circling lower and lower, he can place the item right where he wants it on the ground. It really works. Except," he said, turning to Nate, "what if they don't unsnap it?"

"Hmm. I have to work on that," said Nate. "We need some kind of an automatic release."

Once Nate developed his automatic release for the gifts, he was ready to make the first delivery to the Aucas. He and Ed McCully prepared a small aluminum cooking pot with some buttons and coarse rock salt inside. To this they attached several brightly colored ribbon streamers.

Then they climbed into the yellow Piper Cruiser.

"Clear," Nate called.

"Clear," responded a child's high-pitched yell from outside. Nate turned to check that little Steve was safely away from the plane. The boy stood with his back against the weathered repair shed about ten yards away. He waved vigorously to his dad.

Nate grinned and waved back. "Ain't that some kid?" he said. "He loves planes almost as much as I do."

"Either that or he loves the person inside," Ed said with a knowing nod of his head.

Nate hit the starter button. The prop ground around two or three times, and then the engine coughed to life. *Thug-a-thug-thug. Brrrrr,* it roared, shaking the whole plane as though it had a chill.

Soon the yellow Piper began wobbling from side to side as it rolled slowly across the rough grass toward the gravel airstrip. Nate was grateful to have such a good airstrip out in the middle of the jungle. Shell Mera had been built by the Shell Oil Company and then abandoned when it was no longer needed. The missionaries had obtained permission to make it their headquarters.

Nate and Ed had been in the air for about twenty minutes when Nate put the plane into a steep bank and pointed down with his finger. "There they are," he said.

Through the morning mists, Ed could see the thatched roofs of the communal houses and several native people running around. But as they circled lower, everyone seemed to have disappeared. "Where'd they go?" asked Ed.

Nate frowned. "I don't know. Maybe they got scared."

"We'd better let the gift down and get out of here. When they find it, they'll be more curious next time."

Ed opened the door and let the kettle slowly down on the line as Nate circled over the village.

"How about putting it down on that sandbar near the river," said Ed. "If you try to drop it in the village, it could catch on one of the houses and do some damage. That wouldn't build very much good-will."

As they swung the gift kettle toward the sandbar, a boy sprinted down the path from the village, reaching up for it. "Hey, there's someone," said Ed.

"Yeah. I think I saw him last time," said Nate.

"How can you tell from up here?" asked Ed. "It's not as though he's wearing some bright red shirt that you can easily recognize."

Both men laughed because all Aucas wore the same costume . . . nothing!

"But I still think it's the same kid," said Nate.

And then the kettle with its bright ribbons touched down right where he had aimed it. No sooner had it landed than the boy picked it up and raced back to the village.

"Well, that's it," Nate grinned as he rolled the plane out of its bank and started climbing. "Our first Gospel message by sign language."

"Yeah," said Ed. "I wonder what they think. How much do you think they know about the outside world?"

Nate shrugged. "We know they've seen planes before. Those oil company planes used to fly over this area all the time. But that doesn't mean much."

A week later they made a second gift trip. This time they delivered a machete, and the Aucas didn't hide. They had caught on quickly and were waiting for the drop. But Nate and Ed's aim was not so good, and the machete splashed into the river.

A moment later, an Auca man waded in and retrieved it. Soon half a dozen men were examining it on the bank.

Ed was so excited that he opened the door and yelled down to them, waving his arms wildly. "Hello," he said. "We are friends!"

"Get back in here before you fall," said Nate. "They can't hear you from up here. Besides, even if they could, they can't understand English!"

"I know," Ed said as he pulled his head back in and closed the door. "But I thought they might at least get the idea that I was *trying* to be friendly."

When the two missionaries returned to Shell Mera, they heard some disturbing news. Ed and Marilou McCully actually lived closer to the Aucas than any of the other missionaries. They lived in the small Quechuan village of Arajuno. During the last few days some of the local Quechuan Indians had discovered Auca tracks in the surrounding jungle.

Ed frowned and looked at Nate. "Do you think the Aucas are spying on us? If so, what does that mean?"

Nate shrugged and smiled good-naturedly. "Maybe it just means that the Aucas are as eager for direct contact with us as we are with them."

The Quechua Indians, however, were far more worried. They thought the Aucas were preparing for an attack. Ed decided to make a model of the plane to hang outside his house in Arajuno so that if any Aucas were spying on them, they would know that he was one of the gift-givers.

Each week the missionaries made another visit to the Aucas, delivering gifts they hoped would demonstrate their friendly intentions. Sometimes it was another kettle or an ax or an article of clothing.

Sometimes they flew low over the houses so the Indians could clearly see them in the plane. And sometimes they tied an empty basket onto the end of the line, hoping the Aucas might return a gift. If they returned a gift, agreed the missionaries, that would almost be proof that the Aucas, too, intended to be friendly.

While Nate was making plane contact with the Aucas, Jim Elliot had gone to work with Rachel Saint and the Auca woman, Dayuma, in order to learn some Auca words. "On your next trip," Jim said to Nate, "take me with you, and I'll speak to them through a loudspeaker in their own language and tell them we are friends."

Everyone agreed that was a good idea, and on the next flight, Jim Elliot went along and yelled into the microphone, "We like you. We are your friends."

Around and around they flew over the Auca village, broadcasting the same message as the Indians spun slowly like toy tops with their hands held up to shield their eyes from the sun as they gazed up at the airplane.

"Do you think they understand?" Jim asked when they leveled out to fly back home.

"The Lord only knows," Nate said with a shrug. "At least they don't disappear into the jungle anymore."

"Which must mean they aren't afraid," added Jim hopefully.

"Oh, they're not afraid. They haven't been for a long time," said Nate. "They are always eager to come out and get whatever we bring—whether it's a machete, ax, cooking pot, clothes, or whatever. As you could see, some of them are even wearing a shirt or a pair of pants that we've dropped. But what they really understand about us is an entirely different question."

The next time the missionary families got together to pray and plan, Jim Elliot said, "I've learned from this Dayuma woman that the only 'writing' the Aucas make are notches on trees to mark a path or tell someone they have been there. Rachel says that when we translate the Bible into the Auca language, we should call it 'God's Carving.' But I've got another idea. Let's put five notches on a stick to represent the five of us. Then let's tie five photographs—one of each of us men—to the stick and deliver it with the next flyover. That way they'll begin to know us."

"Great idea," the others agreed.

"I think we are almost ready for 'first contact,'" said Jim.

# Chapter 5

# Word From a Lost Sister

ONE NIGHT NIWA WOKE UP to the sounds of arguing. He sat up in his hammock rubbing his eyes. The fire was very low, but the voices were harsh and angry.

It took Niwa a few moments to figure out who was arguing. He quickly recognized his mother's voice as she stood under the eave of their thatched-roof house talking to some man.

"Go away," said his mother. "You cannot have Gimari. She is only a child. Besides, you already have too many wives."

"How can I have too many wives?" the man's voice said. "That's like me saying you have too many clay pots. You have as many as you want, as many as you can use. Besides, Ipa is my only wife now."

Niwa knew who the man was now. He recognized the voice. Nankiwi was a very cruel man who killed people whenever they crossed his wishes.

"Ipa may be your only wife *now*," said Niwa's mother, "but that is because you already killed your second wife. Seeing you might kill her, too, why should I let my daughter marry you?"

"So what? Not liking them, you sometimes break your clay pots, and then you go make more."

Niwa pushed the cool end of a log into the fire with his toe, causing the flames to flare up and give more light. He looked over to his sister Gimari's hammock. She was sitting there pulling on the decorative round plug in her earlobe and grinning at Nankiwi.

"Quit flirting with him," said Niwa in a harsh whisper.

"Tend your own cooking pot." His sister was an older teenager and thought she should be able to do as she pleased.

By this time, their uncle, who was the man of the communal house, woke up and staggered sleepily over to see what the disturbance was all about. After listening a few minutes to the argument, he said, "Go away, you greedy pig. You have more children than you can feed already. Gimari is going to marry Dyumi. He is a much better man and has no wife."

"No, I'm not," snapped Gimari from the shadows.

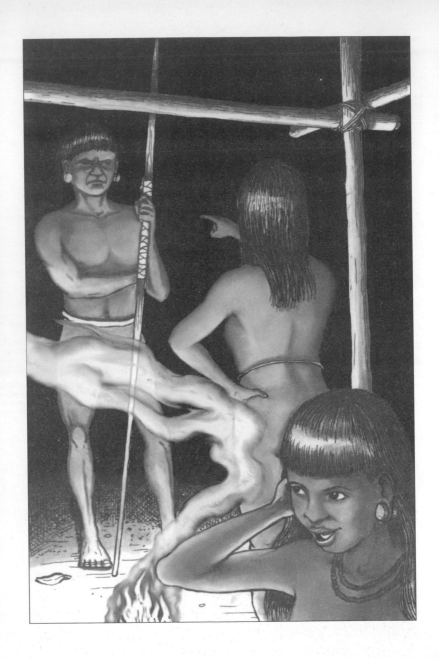

"And you can't make me."

"There, you hear?" said Nankiwi. "Seeing I want her, she has already chosen me."

A movement to Niwa's right caught his eye. It was his older brother, Nampa, moving in a crouched position along the outside edge of their house, working his way to the corner. Though most Auca houses had no walls, a woven bamboo mat hung from this corner of Niwa's house. It made a wall that concealed Nampa's movements from Nankiwi's sight. As Niwa watched, moonlight gleamed on the polished shaft of Nampa's spear.

Niwa glanced back at Nankiwi. He, too, carried a spear. Men seldom went anywhere without one. But Nankiwi leaned on his like it was a walking stick, with the point in the air and the other end on the ground. Nankiwi was not expecting an attack. On the other hand, he was a powerful hunter. If he reacted quickly enough, Nampa wouldn't have a chance.

As Niwa watched, Nankiwi changed his position, turning his body to face the corner of the house around which Nampa would come. It was an adjustment that Nampa couldn't see, but it meant that he would not even have the advantage of surprise.

Niwa had to warn his brother, but how? Finally, in desperation, he called out loudly, "Nampa, come in here and make Gimari stop flirting!"

It worked. His brother's arm that held the spear dropped to his side. His shoulders sagged in disappointment, and he came into the house. "Why did you do that?" he growled through angry, clenched teeth.

"Because he would see you," Niwa whispered.

Nampa glanced toward where the three adults continued to argue. He could see that Niwa was right, that his brother probably had saved his life, but he was still angry.

Finally, Nankiwi left, calling back curses and threats to the family. "I'll have that girl. Just you wait and see."

"I'll be killing you if you try it," responded Niwa's uncle.

The next few days, the fight over Gimari created so much tension the villagers forgot about the visits of the woodbee. Every day when the men went out hunting there was speculation among the women at home about whether Nampa would try to kill Nankiwi or whether Nankiwi would kill the girl's uncle. Of course, so much tension among the men ruined their hunting, and they brought home very little game. That, in turn, made the women angry.

By this time, Niwa's friend Moipa had pretty much recovered from the spear wound he had received from the Downrivers. One morning when Niwa, Dabu, and Moipa went up to the clay hill to play, they got to talking about the tension over Niwa's sister, Gimari. While they scooped up water with gourds and threw it on the hill to make it slick enough to slide down, Moipa said, "If your mother and uncle don't want Gimari to marry Nankiwi, why don't they just marry her to Dyumi?"

Suddenly, the solution seemed so obvious.

Marriage among the Aucas was a very simple matter. All that was involved was announcing to the village that a wedding was going to take place. Then at a dance, or maybe just sitting around the fire, someone would take the man's hand while another person would take the woman's hand and they would put them together. The joining of hands in this public and formal manner meant the two were married.

With relief at discovering such a simple answer, Niwa enjoyed the morning sliding down the mud hill and splashing in the river.

But shortly after they returned home, the woodbee came, and Niwa forgot all about suggesting the idea to his mother.

After dropping its bundle of gifts, the woodbee circled low over the village, and suddenly all the people could hear a voice speaking to them from the noisy creature.

*"Biti miti punimupa!"* said the voice from the woodbee. *"Biti miti punimupa!"*

All the people looked at one another. The words were not pronounced properly and were very hard to understand. Finally, someone figured them out and shouted to everyone else, "Speaking from the sky, the woodbee is saying, 'I like you! I like you!' "

"Yes," agreed someone else. "It is saying, 'I like you!' What a stupid thing for an insect to say."

*49*

Everyone nodded and agreed, and then they broke into laughter. Why would a woodbee be saying, "I like you"? It was the strangest thing they had ever heard.

Niwa stood with the other village people looking up into the sky. He put his hand up to shade his eyes from the bright sun and watched the woodbee as it went around and around making the same stupid comments. Whoever heard of a woodbee saying, "I like you"? How could an insect speak? How could it *like* the people on the ground?

"Do you think that the woodbee speaks to the *cowodi* who ride in its belly?" asked Moipa.

"Who can see such a thing?" said Niwa. "They are very strange creatures. They are not like the bumble-bees we play with."

It was common for Auca children to catch bumble-bees—carefully, without getting stung—and tie a long, thin strand of palm fiber to them. Then they would fly the bees around while holding on to the other end of the thread. It was great sport, and it led them to think that they knew everything about bees. Certainly bees didn't speak.

Just then Niwa's parrot flew from its perch inside the house and landed on Niwa's shoulder. The feathers on the parrot's wings had been trimmed so it wouldn't escape, so it didn't fly very well, and when it landed, it often dug in its claws until it got its balance.

"Ouch!" yelled Niwa.

The parrot bobbed its head and said, *"Biti miti*

*punimupa! Biti miti punimupa!*" "I like you! I like you!"

Everyone laughed.

"There," said Niwa, "some creatures *can* talk!"

"But insects can't speak, no matter how big they are," said Niwa's aunt, Mintaka. "It must be a trick of the *cowodi.*" She spoke with absolute confidence. "They want to trap us."

Several people nodded in agreement. It was the only logical explanation.

"I still think we should move the village," said Gikita.

A week later, the woodbee came again. Niwa went out with some of the other villagers to get the gift. This time it was a bundle of clothes, and they eagerly tore it open, passing around the brightly colored shirts and pants.

Inside was a stick carefully wrapped in shiny gray and white square leaves. Gikita was among those who had come out to retrieve the gift. He tore the square leaves off the stick and threw them into a nearby fire. They curled up and soon burst into flames. Niwa could see that the stick had five notches carved in it, and he realized that it was a message, but Gikita didn't seem to know what it meant. After looking it over and turning it this way and that, he tossed it aside and put on his new red shirt.

Niwa walked over to look at the stick. If it was a

carved message, what did it mean? He picked it up and took it back to his house. "Mother, this came from the woodbee. I think it means something good. Shall I take it to Karea, the witch doctor?"

"What do you want with an old stick?" said Gimari, who was weaving an armband that she said was for her wedding to Nankiwi—no matter what anyone said.

Their mother, Akawo, studied the stick for a long time. Then she said, "It is not necessary to take it to Karea. I can hear what it means. It is from your sister Dayuma. She is telling me she is alive. See, the five notches stand for my five daughters. Disappearing eight years ago, I have never given up hope for my Dayuma. Now I see she is alive!"

"This *is* good news," agreed Niwa. "Do you think she is coming home?"

Niwa's mother frowned and shook her head. "I hear the *cowodi* are cannibals, but maybe not all of them. At least they did not eat my Dayuma. But who can see if she is coming home?"

"If they did not eat Dayuma," Gimari said defiantly, "then, not letting me marry Nankiwi, I, too, will go to them."

"No! You wouldn't dare," cried Akawo. "To lose one daughter has been too much. I almost died of grief. Now that she has sent me a message, my heart is full of joy. You wouldn't dare run off, too."

All that week Niwa thought about the white men who rode in the belly of the yellow woodbee. If Dayuma was living with the *cowodi* and was sending them messages, they should return a message to her. But what should it be?

Finally, Niwa hit on an idea. He would send Dayuma a gift. He would send her his finest possession. He would send her his pet parrot.

# Chapter 6

# Palm Beach

ED McCULLY GRABBED for the metal brace inside the Piper's windshield to steady himself as the plane tipped violently to the left and then dove toward the ground, twisting in a tight spiral.

"Yikes," he yelled at Nate Saint. "What are you doing?"

"Look down there," Nate said excitedly as he pointed at the river below them.

"Where else can I look? You're heading right toward it. Don't you think you could take it a little easier? I almost lost my breakfast—and I didn't even *have* any this morning."

"Sorry," said Nate as he leveled the plane out. "But look—I think we found our 'Palm Beach.'" He then put the plane into a gentle right turn.

Ed looked out his side window and studied the river below. The two were on their way back from their weekly gift drop to the Aucas. "You mean that sandbar down there?" said Ed. "But it's so small. You'll never land this thing on that."

"Let's go down and see. I've been searching this river every time we've flown out here, and that's the best I've seen. There are so many hairpin turns in that river that there are very few beaches long enough to land on. The heavy rains last week must have really churned up the river and laid down that nice-looking sandbar."

Ed kept his grip on the brace inside the windshield as the plane again descended, though this time Nate's spiral was more gentle. As the plane came down just forty or fifty feet above the treetops and lined up with the sandbar, Ed said, "We'll never make it, Nate. Those trees on this end are too high. You can't drop down over them soon enough to hit this end of the beach."

"Don't be too sure," said Nate. "Watch this."

Suddenly, as they came over the last tall tree, the plane turned to the side while continuing its forward direction and began to slip down rapidly toward the sand along the river. The maneuver created a sickening sensation of skidding sideways out of control. Then at the last moment, Nate straightened it out, and they skimmed along about ten feet above the beach.

When they got to the other end, Nate pulled back on the stick and applied the power. Up the little Piper zoomed and settled into a gentle left-hand turn. "How'd it look out your side?" he called.

"I don't know! I was too scared to pay attention."

"Hey, you're supposed to be watching out for logs and sticks in the sand to see if it's safe to touch down," said Nate. A moment later he said, "We'll go back and buzz the sandbar again. I sure wish we weren't going with the wind. It'd be so much safer landing and taking off into the wind, but there's no way we can come in from the other direction."

This time Ed forced himself to watch his side of the beach as it raced past outside his window. He didn't see any sticks or logs or sharp banks, and he told Nate so.

"That's good," said Nate. "How long do you think it is?"

"Who knows?" said Ed. *Certainly not long enough for a landing,* he thought as he remembered how quickly they had gone from one end to the other.

"Well, we'll check it. There're some paper bags on the floor behind your seat. Do you see them?"

Ed turned around. "These with flour in 'em?"

"Yeah. But it's not flour; it's powdered paint. Now, this time when we buzz the beach, I want you to open the door and drop one *exactly* when I tell you to. Then get ready and drop the second one when I tell you. We'll be flying at a steady speed, and the second bag should bomb the beach two hundred yards

*56*

from where the first one hit. That way we can estimate how long the beach is."

The "bomb" run worked well, showing that the beach was about 230 yards long. "Good," said Nate as they flew around one more time. "We can make it if the sand isn't too soft."

"How can you tell if it's firm enough or not?"

"We'll just touch our wheels down lightly without actually landing. If they don't sink in too much, we're okay."

"And if they do?"

"Well," said Nate, "they could grab and tip us up on our nose, maybe even flip us over on our back, depending on how fast we are going. But . . ." He was just coming into his final approach where he had to slip the plane down over the trees, and he bit his lip in concentration.

As Nate gently let the plane down, the wheels kissed the ground. The plane lurched slightly as the they dug into sand, but Nate compensated quickly by pulling back on the stick and adding a little power. The plane broke free. Then he set the wheels down again. This time they rolled along smoothly for thirty or forty yards before he pushed the throttle forward and took off again.

"There you have it," said Nate as they climbed up into the blue sky. "I think we've found ourselves a landing strip—not too far from our Aucas, either—if the river doesn't flood again and wash it all away."

❖ ❖ ❖ ❖

Later that December afternoon when the two scouts walked into the mission house at Shell Mera, they had big grins on their faces. "I think we've found our 'Palm Beach,'" announced Ed.

"Your what?" said Elisabeth Elliot as the other missionaries gathered around.

"Our 'Palm Beach,'" said Ed. "You know, a nice resort like Palm Beach, California, or Palm Beach, Florida—a nice place to invite the Aucas to visit for our first contact."

"Yeah," added Nate. "And it looks pretty good."

Jim Elliot stepped forward and handed both men a glass of chilled fruit juice. "Where is it?" he asked.

With his free hand, Nate removed his baseball cap and scratched his head. "I figure it's no more than about eight miles as the crow flies from their village. But with the hills and all, it might be a ten- or twelve-mile hike through the jungle—half a day's journey. Not bad, huh?"

Excited, they described their adventure of testing the landing strip and the ideas they had already been forming for where they should set up camp and how to get the Aucas to come see them.

"It's going to take several trips to ferry in all the supplies we'll need," said Nate. "And the big challenge will be for the first guy I leave there alone. If the Aucas are watching that place because of all our landings and takeoffs, an unarmed man wouldn't have a chance if they decided to attack."

"You're not suggesting we take guns, are you?" asked Jim.

"Not against the Aucas," said Nate, "but what about animals? There are jaguars and anacondas and crocodiles out there. I can't see going in without some protection." The idea of facing a huge anaconda snake that could crush a man to death made him shiver, and he tried to put the thought out of his mind. "And what about hunting?" he said. "If there's any problem flying supplies in and out, we'll need to get our own food."

"And if the Aucas did attack," Pete Fleming said, "a shot or two in the air might scare them off. That would be better for them—and certainly for us—than if someone got killed."

Jim nodded. "I guess you're right."

Finally, it was decided that they would take a couple of handguns for protection against wild animals and a shotgun for hunting small game. But they would always keep them hidden. They made a pledge to each other that—even if they were attacked by the Aucas—they would not shoot at the Indians. The most they would do would be to fire a warning shot into the air, hoping the noise would scare away any attackers.

"In that case," said Elisabeth, "you better make sure they intend to be friendly before you go in."

The following week after Nate and Ed lowered their gift package down to the eager Indians, Ed said, "Hold on, Nate. Don't pull up so fast. I think the line is caught. Either that, or someone's holding on to it."

Nate kept the plane flying in the tight, level circle that allowed the bottom of the line to remain steady.

"Okay, now it's free," said Ed as he started to reel it in. "No. Wait a minute. There's something on the end of it." With eager excitement, he shouted over the noise of the engine. "They've attached something to it."

"You're right," said Nate. "It looks like a package. I think it is a return gift!"

"Hallelujah!" said Ed. "This has gotta be a big breakthrough."

They did not try to reel the package up into the plane for fear that a strong blast of air from the propeller would cause it to tangle in the tail. Instead, the package dangled hundreds of feet below the plane as they flew slowly home. When they arrived, they set it down at the end of the landing strip in just the same manner they delivered gifts to the Indians. Then Ed cut the line at the plane's end, and they came around to land.

When they got to the package, it turned out to be a bamboo cage covered with cloth. Inside the cage was a beautiful parrot munching on a piece of banana.

"We have friendly Aucas!" Nate announced to the other missionaries who came running. He held up the cage. "And this is the proof. They're giving us gifts now."

Ed McCully nodded soberly. "I think we're ready to go in."

Later that evening as Nate Saint tucked his son Steve into bed he said, "How'd you like to have that red and green parrot I brought home today?"

"Boy, would I," said Steve. "He's great!"

"That way, every time I'm away, you can play with him and remember me."

"Thanks, Dad." The little boy threw his arms around his father's neck and gave him a big hug. Then he went to sleep, dreaming about parrots, airplanes, and his dad.

## Chapter 7

# The Runaway Couple

AKAWO WAS SO EXCITED by the idea that her lost daughter was sending gifts to her in the woodbee that she asked Niwa to build a platform high in a tree so the next time the woodbee flew over the village he could look inside. "Maybe she's inside, riding with the *cowodi*," said Akawo. "Seeing her, maybe you can wave to her."

Niwa chose an old balsa tree at the edge of the garden. Its top had been knocked off years before by lightning, but it was still the tall-est tree around. For three days he hacked steps in the side of the tree with a machete, and then he carried up stout poles to build a platform at the top, tying them in place with tough vines. Finally, the platform was finished, and he was ready for the woodbee's next visit.

When he heard its droning sound in the distance, he quickly scrambled up the tree to the platform. The platform was so high that the slightest breeze caused it to sway. Whenever that happened, Niwa did not look down for fear of getting dizzy.

In just a few moments the yellow woodbee swooped low over Tiwaeno. Niwa had thought he would be just as high as the woodbee and could look right inside its belly. But he wasn't. It was still much higher. He could see the two white men, however, and he waved eagerly to them. They waved back to him, but there was no sign of Dayuma.

Some of the villagers had seen Niwa tie his parrot cage onto the vine hanging from the woodbee the week before, and it had caused much debate. "Why send the *cowodi* gifts?" they asked. Niwa explained that he didn't believe that they were cannibals. Why not make friends with them? But others disagreed. They still mistrusted the *cowodi*. On the other hand, trading—even with one's enemies—made good business sense if you were careful. Besides, it might encourage the white men to send them more machetes and axes. And those were the items they really wanted. Who needed those foolish clothes and carved sticks wrapped in square gray leaves?

From his perch up in the tree, Niwa watched as Kimo, one of the village men, attached a gift to the long vine hanging from the woodbee. Niwa knew what it was—a headband with many feathers that Kimo had been making all week. The woodbee pulled it up and then began to talk again. To Niwa it sounded like the same foolish message: *"Biti miti punimupa! Biti miti punimupa!"* "I like you! I like you!"

Finally, the woodbee circled higher and flew away across the jungle. Niwa had not seen his older sister Dayuma. He came down from the tree and walked slowly to report to his mother.

"If Dayuma doesn't ride in the woodbee," she reasoned after hearing what Niwa had to say, "then she must live in the place where the woodbee comes from. Could you see where it went? Can you hear where it makes its nest? If she can't come to us in the woodbee, then we must make a journey to her."

Niwa shrugged. The woodbee had flown away, far across the jungle. Niwa felt certain that they could never make such a long trip. However, when Niwa explained this to his mother, she disagreed. "That's not true. Some of our people have gone to where the *cowodi* live. They have seen the woodbees land and crawl into their nest. We, too, must make such a trip."

That evening Gikita confronted Kimo for sending the *cowodi* a gift. "It is foolish," he said. "First this boy, Niwa, sends something. Now you send something. And today we have more foolish talk from that yellow insect. I believe it is all a trick. What if your gifts brings the *cowodi* right here to our village of Tiwaeno? Then what will we do?"

Kimo frowned scornfully and said, "If the *cowodi* come to Tiwaeno, we will kill them."

"Not understanding, you think it will be as easy as swatting a mosquito!" scoffed Gikita. "Have you forgotten so soon what happened the last time we killed *cowodi*? More came with their long sticks that bang. They killed many Aucas before we could escape into the jungle. We do not want them here!"

During all this talk, Nankiwi, the man who wanted Niwa's sister, just listened with a gleam in his eye. He was usually the first person to encourage killing, so why was he silent? Niwa wondered. Niwa did not trust him. He was planning something.

The next time Niwa heard the woodbee buzzing in the sky, he again climbed into his perch to watch it deliver its gift. However, this time it did not lower anything on the end of a vine. Instead, it just circled around making strange sounds that the Aucas had figured was its attempt to speak. In addition to saying, "I like you," it seemed to be saying, "Come tomorrow. Come tomorrow." But what could that possibly mean?

Niwa watched as the yellow woodbee flew off over the jungle. Suddenly, he realized that it was going in a slightly different direction than it had the previous time. And then, as he watched, it did a most remarkable thing. It dropped down and disappeared!

Niwa waited, expecting it to rise again like it did

when it flew low over his village. But it did not rise, and he could no longer hear its buzzing. He thought for a moment. It had gone down into the valley where the Curaray River ran. But it did not come up. That could mean only one thing. It must have a nest there. It must have landed in its nest. Maybe it had *cowodi* in its nest. If it did, they were very close.

As he climbed down, he debated with himself whether to tell anyone about what he'd seen. Surely his mother would want to go see if Dayuma was with them. Niwa was not sure that was a good idea.

In the village he found much turmoil. Everyone had heard the woodbee saying, "Come tomorrow." But where? they wondered. And there had been no gift this time. Were the *cowodi* angry? Was it a trick to get them to wander off into the jungle forever?

Finally, Niwa could contain his knowledge no longer. "No," he said. "It is not a trick. The woodbee is not far away. It has a new nest along the Curaray. I saw it go down into the valley and not come up again. It landed there."

"You saw this? Where? Tell us all the details!" his neighbors demanded as they gathered around him. And so Niwa explained all he had seen—how the woodbee had flown far away across the jungle the last time it had visited them, but this time it had landed nearby.

Akawo was excited. Just as Niwa had thought, she was certain that the woodbee had brought her daughter Dayuma. "Now she will be coming," Akawo said. "My daughter is coming home. My daughter is coming home."

"Ha!" spat Gikita. "You think your daughter is coming home. What's coming are the cannibals. We must flee Tiwaeno!"

Niwa had not anticipated this reaction. Some people were so frightened that they were ready to grab their hammocks, pots, and blowguns and run into the jungle. Others began talking of going to kill the *cowodi* before they had a chance to attack them.

As the village members argued, Niwa noticed Gimari and Nankiwi secretly talking with each other. Suddenly, Gimari stepped forward and announced to her mother, "If you don't let me marry Nankiwi," she shouted so everyone could hear, "then I'll run away and go to the *cowodi.*"

"No," wailed Akawo. "They will kill you!"

Niwa was confused. One moment, his mother seemed to believe that Dayuma had survived and was living well with the *cowodi*. Then, the next moment, she was convinced that Gimari would be killed if she went to them. What was going on?

Gimari stuck out her lip in a pout like a small child. "Why should I care if they kill me?" she snapped. "What could be worse than living here in Tiwaeno with you?" She marched off into the jungle on the path that led toward the Curaray River.

Seeing his chance to be alone with Gimari, Nankiwi ran after her. And then Niwa saw what was happening. This was all about the ongoing fight over whether Nankiwi would marry Gimari. Everyone in the village knew that Gimari's brother and uncle opposed the marriage. Such a strong disagreement could lead to killing. It almost had already.

Now, at a time of such crisis with the *cowodi* near, who would stop Nankiwi and Gimari if they just ran off together? Maybe later they would come back to the village and be accepted as husband and wife. The village of less than fifty people had only seven adult men left after all the killings among themselves and wars with other Auca groups. The loss of any more men would make it hard for these Aucas to survive. There would not be enough men to hunt, fish, and defend the village. What could anyone do to stop Gimari?

But Akawo was not so ready to give up. As the girl's mother, she also opposed the marriage. "Please," she begged, "someone must go with them so they don't marry. I would go myself, but Nankiwi would kill me. Please, won't someone go?"

"I'll go," offered Niwa.

Everyone laughed. "What good would that do? You could not stop them from marrying," his aunt Mintaka said.

Such words embarrassed Niwa and made him angry. He was not so young and helpless. He would follow anyway. Suppose Gimari did as she had threatened and went to the *cowodi*. He wanted to see them and the woodbee. This could be his chance.

Finally, it was decided that Aunt Mintaka would go after the pair. As an older woman and a relative, she would make a satisfactory chaperone.

❖ ❖ ❖ ❖

Niwa followed his Aunt Mintaka into the jungle, but he kept his distance. Ever since Mintaka had chased him with the machete, he had not trusted her. The jungle had its dangers, as he well knew, but he would not make them worse by being caught alone by her.

By evening, Mintaka had joined up with Gimari and Nankiwi. Niwa spotted them arguing together under a banana tree. Raising his spear high over his head, Nankiwi threatened Mintaka and tried to drive her off, but she wouldn't leave them. Finally, Gimari tried to pull the same trick she had used back at the village. "If I cannot marry Nankiwi, then I will be going to the *cowodi*. I don't care if they kill me."

She started to walk away, but by then, it was getting dark and was much too late to travel. Mintaka and Nankiwi stood there watching her until she turned back and joined them. There was more arguing as they ate bananas and prepared to spend the night, but it was not loud enough for Niwa to catch many of the words.

Without anything to eat, Niwa curled up between the tall roots of a pepper kapok tree and tried to keep warm. Soon he fell asleep.

The next morning he was awakened by more arguing. "Why don't you go home, you old woman," shouted Nankiwi as he and Gimari headed off into the jungle. But Mintaka followed doggedly along a few paces behind.

Niwa hurried to keep them in sight as they wove between the trees and vines. The tallest trees of the rain forest created an upper canopy, filtering out much of the sunlight. Shorter trees created a middle layer of foliage. Where this was thick, very little light reached the forest floor, and the tangle of vines and bushes and plants were thinner, making it possible for Niwa to keep the other three in sight from a distance. But sometimes the upper levels thinned out, and enough sunlight filtered through so that the forest floor was choked with greenery. Then Niwa lost sight of Gimari, Nankiwi, and Mintaka. Fortunately, the same jungle thickness meant it was nearly impossible to go off the trail, and by following it and listening for their voices, he was able to follow.

Throughout the day Gimari and Nankiwi sometimes headed toward the Curaray River—usually after failing to convince Mintaka to leave them alone. Then after a while, they would turn away and head in a new direction. It was obvious to Niwa that Gimari and Nankiwi were more interested in losing Mintaka than in fleeing to the *cowodi*.

Would he ever find the woodbee by following these three?

Finally, by the second evening, when they were very near the Curaray River, another argument broke out. Niwa carefully approached them through a stand of bamboo so he could hear what was being said. "I don't care anymore," he heard Mintaka say. "If you want to marry this crazy man, what's it to me if you ruin your life? But I can't go back to Tiwaeno without you, Gimari, or everyone will see that I have failed in my job. So you just have to put up with me."

At that moment a snake struck at Niwa. He jumped so quickly away from the creature that he fell crashing into the noisy bamboo. Nankiwi heard the noise, turned, and saw him.

Just when Nankiwi was finally getting what he

wanted, Niwa had spoiled it by witnessing Mintaka's giving up. That would never do; Niwa would tell the rest of the village and ruin his plans. The angry man raised his spear and came toward Niwa with hatred in his eyes.

## Chapter 8

# First Contact

WHILE JIM ELLIOT, Pete Fleming, and Roger Youderian were praying on the morning of January 3, 1956, Nate Saint and Ed McCully took off for "Palm Beach." It was the most exciting day of their lives. This is what they had planned and worked for over the last few months.

There were patches of fog lying in the jungle valleys, but when they arrived over the sandbar on the Curaray, it was clear. They had planned to buzz the beach three times before trying to set down, but on the second run, everything felt so right that Nate set the plane down on the sand.

74

They jumped out as soon as the plane rolled to a stop and looked around. This would be their base for meeting the Aucas. This was going to be it. Then Ed went to one end with the movie camera while Nate taxied the plane to the other to take off. They had deliberately not brought any equipment on this first trip so the plane would be as light as possible for its first takeoff. If the plane couldn't make it empty, they would be stuck and have to wait until a rescue team could be organized and travel down the river by canoe. But that would take days.

Nate gunned the engine, stirring up a swirl of dust from the sand and mist from the river. Then he came rumbling toward Ed, bouncing along over the beach.

Ed held the camera steady. Nate was getting closer, but it didn't look like he was moving very fast. Would he gain enough speed to lift off? From his perspective, he couldn't tell. Half the distance was covered, and then the tail came up. The plane was eating up the remaining beach. What would Nate do if he had to give up? Would there be time to stop before he nosed into the river or crashed into the trees on the other side?

And then with relief, Ed saw the wheels lift off the sand.

Nate kept the plane close to the ground to gain speed. Only at the last minute did he pull it up sharply to clear the trees.

On the next flight, Nate brought Jim and Roger so that Ed would not be alone. While Nate returned to pick up supplies, Jim, Roger, and Ed set to work cutting down the tallest trees across the river so there would be a little more safety in takeoff.

Once Nate brought in a radio, some tools, and boards, the three Palm Beachers set to work building a tree house in a tall ironwood tree at the edge of the forest. Later they would build a roof for it with sheets of aluminum.

Finally, after his fifth trip, Nate took off and flew to the Auca village. As he circled, he used the loudspeaker to invite them to come and visit the next day: "I like you. Come tomorrow. Come tomorrow." He said it as clearly as possible in the Auca words that Jim had learned from Nate's sister, Rachel Saint, and the Auca woman called Dayuma.

After that he headed back to the missionary base, where he would spend the night with his family. The next morning, Nate planned to take Pete Fleming and the remaining supplies to Palm Beach.

Hopefully, it would be the day they would make their first contact with the Aucas.

That night, when the lantern had been extinguished and the three missionaries laid down on their platform thirty feet up in the air, Ed McCully said, "Let's pray, boys."

They all agreed, and so with their mosquito netting pulled over them to keep the bugs off, Ed said, "Dear Lord, we want to thank You for our safe arrivals today and for helping us get this little platform put up before dark. Please be with Nate and Pete as they come in tomorrow. And most of all, give us a successful first contact with our Auca friends. Amen."

In spite of their unstable position, they all slept well—except for being awakened in the middle of the night by a horrible scream not far away.

"What's that?" said Jim as he sat up, his heart pounding.

"I don't know," said Ed. "It sounded like a woman screaming, and not far away at that."

Roger coughed a couple times. "It wasn't human," he said. "It was a cat."

"A cat? You mean a jaguar?" asked Jim.

"They roar and growl. I don't think they make that kind of a scream," said Roger.

"What else could it be?" said Jim.

"Maybe a puma—you know, a mountain lion. They scream like that," said Roger. "Where's that flashlight? And who's got the guns?"

"Here's the flashlight, and the shotgun's still down in the plane, but I don't know where the pistols are," said Ed. "By the way, can those big cats climb trees?"

Roger let out a nervous laugh. "You bet they can. Jaguars are especially good climbers . . . and excellent swimmers."

They heard no more sounds from the cat, but the next morning they found its footprints on the beach. It had, indeed, been a puma. After that, they made sure the holstered pistols were available. "But let's keep that shotgun out of sight as much as possible," Jim said. "If the Aucas are spying on us, they might recognize a long gun and be scared off."

The plane arrived shortly after the fog cleared, and all five men eagerly congratulated one another on the new day, the day they hoped to meet their Auca friends.

They passed the morning improving their camp and trying to keep cool in the jungle heat. To escape continual attack from the sweat bees and gnats, they frequently dove into the river, enjoying its cool currents. Jim Elliot also managed to catch a catfish. And each man wrote a note to his wife, which Nate would take back to base when he went for supplies.

From time to time, they took turns yelling at the jungle surrounding them. *"Puinani! Puinani!"* they called in their best approximation of the Auca word meaning "Welcome!"

"I wouldn't be surprised if they were out there watching us right now," said Nate from the tree house, where he was trying to get the radio working. "They're a curious and violent people, but they're not foolish. They probably want to check us out very carefully before coming into camp."

"But what if they haven't even left their village yet?" said Ed. "What if they don't know where we are?"

"Tell you what, as soon as I get this radio working, I'll—hold it a minute. I think I'm getting something." Nate spoke into the microphone. "Shell Mera, Shell Mera. This is Palm Beach. Do you read me?"

There was a lot of static in Nate's earphones, and

then Marj's voice came through loud and clear. They talked a few minutes, and then Nate announced to the other guys with a grin, "We're back in touch with civilization."

Wednesday passed without any contact. When Nate took off that afternoon, he flew over the Auca village before heading home to deliver the notes from the other men and get more supplies.

Early Thursday he returned to Palm Beach, but that day also passed without any sign of the Aucas. They were getting discouraged.

Then on Friday morning, a little before noon as the five missionaries were calling out words of welcome toward the forest, they suddenly heard someone call back from across the river. In a few moments three Indians stepped out of the jungle, a man and two women.

Cautiously, the two groups approached each other, the missionaries saying, *"Puinani! Puinani!"*

The Auca man responded with a long paragraph that none of the missionaries understood, but the man seemed to be friendly, so they were delighted. The young girl kept saying something that seemed like a question, the same question with the same words, but the missionaries couldn't understand even one word of it.

"Try some of the words Rachel taught you," Nate said to Jim.

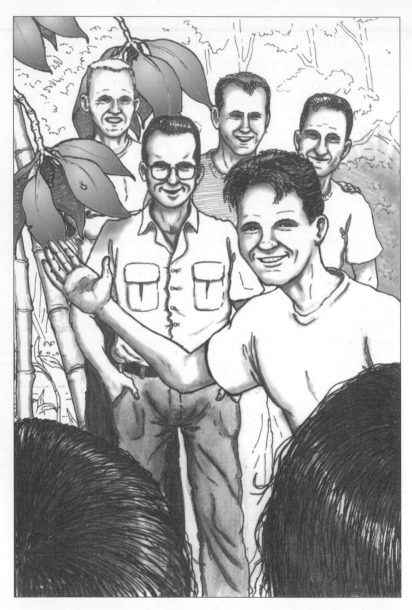

Jim tried the word he thought meant to eat, but
the Indians expressed no recognition until he made

signs with his hands of putting something in his mouth. Then they smiled and repeated something over and over that none of the white men recognized.

The younger woman ran off into the jungle and then returned in a few minutes with a handful of large, wiggling grubs. She popped one in her mouth and offered the others to the white men.

*"Biti miti punimupa!"* Jim said, trying the phrase they had been broadcasting from the loudspeaker for many days that they thought meant, "I like you!"

The Aucas laughed in an embarrassed manner as they covered their mouths with their hands and grinned to each other. Finally, the older woman said the words back to them. *"Biti miti punimupa!"* But it sounded quite different than when Jim had said it.

"We've been saying these things all wrong," Ed blurted. "What if they haven't understood any of the things we've been saying?"

"Oh, I don't think that's true," said Nate. "Obviously they did figure out that we were trying to say 'I like you,' and they were just correcting us."

"Obviously, my eye!" said Ed. "How do we know? We don't know. What they said clearly sounds different than what we were saying, so how do we know what it means?"

The more they experimented with words and phrases they thought they knew, the more they realized how difficult the Auca language was. "What if that woman Rachel is working with isn't even an Auca?" ventured Pete. "Maybe she's from some unknown tribe that's just related to the Aucas."

"No, no," said Jim. "Dayuma is Auca. There's no question about that. They are all from the same tribe. Look at how their hair is cut—bangs, right across the forehead. Look at how they are dressed— nothing. And look at those round balsa wood plugs in their earlobes. Dayuma is Auca."

Suddenly, the older woman became very excited. She came right up to Jim and spoke very fast, gesturing with her hands, asking him some kind of question.

"Listen," said Ed. "She's saying 'Dayuma.' She's asking something about Dayuma. They know who she is."

"Dayuma, Dayuma," Jim nodded eagerly. "Dayuma. Yes, *Sí!*" he slipped into Spanish. "Dayuma, Dayuma."

Finally, they had managed some kind of communication, some kind of connection. But what did it mean?

As they considered their success, they were both excited and worried. On the one hand, these people obviously knew Dayuma. On the other, they had not created nearly as much connection with the Aucas as they had thought they had by shouting to them with the loudspeaker. That meant there was not as much assurance of friendship as they had hoped. Still, this first contact was going smoothly. The Indians seemed friendly. Their prayers seemed to have been answered.

The Aucas seemed interested in several things the white men showed them, such as rubber bands, brightly colored balloons, a yo-yo, and a model of the Piper Cruiser. After a while the Auca man wandered over to the plane and looked it over curiously. "Here, here," said Nate. "This is how the door opens, and I get in"—as though the man could suddenly understand English.

And maybe he understood more than they realized because he suddenly put his machete into the plane and indicated with hand motions that he wanted to go for a ride. He was so insistent that Nate finally took him up. In a few minutes they were circling over the Auca village. The man pushed open the window and yelled and waved to the obviously amazed Indians on the ground. *This is fantastic,* thought Nate. *His friends and relatives will see him and realize that it is safe to visit us.*

On his way back to Palm Beach, he radioed Marj and reported the good news of a successful first contact.

That afternoon, the missionaries shared lemonade and hamburgers with mustard with the Aucas. Some of the food the Indians obviously liked, and some they spat out. All the time the missionaries took pictures, and the Aucas did not seem at all anxious or even curious about the camera.

Finally, when evening came, the man and the younger woman wandered off into the jungle.

"Hey," said Ed. "Don't let 'em go. What if they don't come back?"

"What can we do?" responded Pete. "They aren't our prisoners. Having come once and had a good visit, they're more likely to come back. Besides, it looks like the older woman is going to stay."

She was curling up by the fire with her feet toward it. She gave every appearance that she was going to sleep, so the missionaries climbed up into their tree house and thanked God for such a remarkable day.

But when morning came, she, too, had departed, just disappeared into the jungle without a trace.

"Not to worry," announced Jim, stretching happily as the bright morning sun rose over the trees. "They'll be back. I'm sure of it."

"Me too," Ed agreed. "I think they just went to tell the rest of the village to come for a visit."

But all that day—Saturday—no one showed up, and the five men began to worry whether the contact had been broken. Finally, Nate announced, "I'm gonna give them five more minutes. If they don't show up, I'll fly over the village and see what's happening."

Five minutes came and went, then ten and twenty. Finally, Nate and Pete climbed into the Piper and took off. To their surprise, when they buzzed down over the village, as Nate had done many times before, the Aucas ran into the jungle or hid in their houses. Pete dropped a blanket and a pair of pants from the plane's drop line to reassure them of their continuing friendship.

"Something funny is going on," Nate said when they landed. "I don't know what it is, but they are acting differently. It was almost as though they were frightened of us."

On a second flight, Nate saw the man who had visited them at "Palm Beach." He was standing by the young boy who often climbed the platform and waved to them. *He probably wants an airplane ride, too,* thought Nate as he headed home. He planned to deliver their exposed film and spend the night with his family that night at Shell Mera and return to Palm Beach the next morning with fresh supplies.

That night, back at Palm Beach, the four remaining missionaries prayed about the next day. "Lord," Jim prayed, "we ask that there would be another visit tomorrow, and that the Aucas would give us a clear invitation to take a trip to visit their village."

When Jim had finished praying, Ed said, "What a way to celebrate Sunday! Wouldn't that be great?" Then they pulled their mosquito netting over themselves and fell asleep in their jungle tree house.

The next morning, on his way to Palm Beach, Nate flew over the village again. It seemed nearly empty, but as he flew from there to Palm Beach, he saw about ten Aucas on a trail that was obviously headed toward the Curaray River. "Hallelujah!" he shouted, even though there was no one in the plane with him.

But when he landed, he shouted to the four campers, "This is it, guys! They're on their way!"

The men eagerly made plans for the arrival of their guests, and about noon the missionaries called their base by radio. "Today's the day, girls!" they said to their wives. "Pray for us. The Aucas should be here in a couple hours. We'll call you back at four-thirty with our report."

Excitement lifted everyone's spirits at both Shell Mera and Palm Beach.

But at four-thirty, the radio on Marj Saint's desk at Shell Mera remained silent.

# Chapter 9

## "Cannibals"

WHEN NIWA SAW THE HATRED in the eyes of Nankiwi, he ran for his life. The spear that Nankiwi held at the ready was no idle threat. He had killed before, and he would do it again. Niwa had just witnessed Mintaka give up on keeping Nankiwi and Gimari unmarried. If the village heard about that, Nankiwi's plans could be ruined.

Panting hard, Niwa turned on to a side trail and turned again at the next branch and the next. He knew he was still headed generally toward Tiwaeno and away from the Curaray River, where the woodbee had landed. But by the time he finally stopped running, he had no idea where he was.

He tried to control his breathing and listen. If Nankiwi was still chasing him, he would have to make some noise. He heard the bark of a couple of red howler monkeys in the trees above and the *squawk, squawk* of some toucan birds, all on top of the symphonic hum of millions of insects and tree frogs. But he didn't hear the thud of Nankiwi's feet on the dirt path or the crash of his strong body plowing through the undergrowth. Maybe the angry man had returned to Gimari.

Nevertheless, Niwa had had enough of spying for one day. He headed home.

Back at Tiwaeno he decided to say nothing about what he had seen and heard. Mintaka was right—let Gimari do as she pleased. If she wanted to marry such an evil man, it would be she who suffered. And as for the woodbee and the *cowodi*, he would find some other time to contact them.

It was typical of the Auca people for his mother to not even ask where he had been when he came splashing across the clear Tiwaeno River and walked—still dripping—into their house. Niwa dipped a big gourd into the pot of sticky manioc and then took the milky drink to his hammock, where he flopped down and gulped the first real meal he'd had in a day and a half.

The next day Niwa heard the drone of the yellow woodbee and ran into the clearing to see it circling over the village. As he watched, his mouth dropped open in astonishment. Instead of two *cowodi* riding in its belly, a familiar brown face was grinning and waving to them as the woodbee flew low over their houses.

"It's Nankiwi! It's Nankiwi!" shouted some of the other children who were jumping with excitement in the clearing. By this time everyone in Tiwaeno was staring at the amazing sight. It was unbelievable! Had the woodbee eaten him? *That would serve Nankiwi right for stealing my sister,* thought Niwa. But the man looked well enough, smiling and waving like he was riding a canoe down the river while everyone else paddled.

That night the remarkable event filled the conversations around every family's cooking fire. Stories of hunting and fishing and killing enemies were forgotten as everyone talked of Nankiwi in the woodbee. As they talked, Nankiwi became something of a hero rather than the most hated man in Tiwaeno.

"Now I have lost two daughters to the *cowodi,*" moaned Akawo. She grasped her arms as though hugging herself and rocked back and forth on a log.

"We could all go visit the *cowodi* at the Curaray," suggested Niwa to cheer up his mother. He was also hoping that he might get to ride in the woodbee. But his mother did not seem to pay any attention to his suggestion, at least not then. However, the next morning Niwa's brother, Nampa, his mother, Akawo, and several other Aucas set out on the trail headed for the Curaray River, and Niwa was with them. He was willing to risk meeting an angry Nankiwi again if there was a chance to ride in the woodbee. Besides, with so much excitement—meeting the *cowodi* and riding in the woodbee—Nankiwi would certainly forget about Niwa spying on him.

But before they got to the river, they ran into Nankiwi and Gimari in the jungle. The two lovers seemed very surprised to see everyone, and Nankiwi stared angrily at Niwa.

Immediately, Nampa ran up to them. "Why are

you out here alone in the jungle with my sister?" he demanded. He raised his spear in preparation to kill Nankiwi.

"Wait, wait. Don't kill me," Nankiwi begged. "We have just escaped the *cowodi*. You are in danger, too."

At that moment, Akawo intervened, pushing herself between the two men. "Having been with the *cowodi*, have you seen my Dayuma?" she said, grabbing Nankiwi by the arm and shaking him.

Nankiwi's eyes darted from one person to the next. Akawo's interruption was his good fortune. Watching him, Niwa could almost read his mind. If Nankiwi could distract Nampa and the others from having found him and Gimari alone in the jungle, he might save his own life. "Oh, good woman," Nankiwi said, "we did not see your dear daughter. Who can see it? We fear that she may have been eaten by the *cowodi*. They are very bad!"

"I don't believe you," said Akawo. "You were in the *cowodi*'s woodbee. They cannot be so bad. Riding up in the air, we saw you."

"Not believing, I also challenge you," snapped Nampa. "Where is Mintaka? We will ask her."

"Yes," said some of the other villagers. "We want to ask Mintaka about Dayuma! Where is she? We do not trust you! Where is Mintaka?"

Nankiwi cocked his head to one side. "I do not hear her," he shrugged. "Mintaka had to flee another way. If the white men didn't catch and eat her, maybe she will be along later." He shook his head vigorously. "No, no. You should all go home. The *cowodi* are no good. There are this many of them." He held up the five fingers of one hand. "They tried to kill us!"

Nankiwi's effort to distract everyone from the fact that they had found him and Gimari alone in the jungle began to work. The mystery of the *cowodi* was too strong. And the fact that some of their own people had actually been with the *cowodi* clouded the villagers' good judgment. All the way home, the people debated whether the white men were cannibals or not.

Niwa trudged along behind everyone, confused. He didn't believe what Nankiwi said, but he hesitated to speak up because he didn't want to draw attention to himself. Better to let Nankiwi forget that Niwa had followed him and Gimari and overheard their secret plans to get married. And Mintaka's disappearance made him feel uncertain. What was the truth?

Finally, Gikita, who was the oldest person in the village, began to review again all the killings that had been committed by outsiders, how they had long sticks that made a loud bang and shot fire that could kill you from as far away as one could see.

By the time the group got home, everyone was ready to go to war. Some people were afraid. Some were angry. But almost everyone agreed that their only chance seemed to be to kill the *cowodi* before the *cowodi* killed them.

"Do they have the fire sticks that go bang?"

asked Kimo, one of the men.

Nankiwi started to nod his head yes, but Gimari spoke up first. "We did not see any fire sticks, but they tried to poison us with *strange* food. We are alive only because we spat it out."

"They tried to poison you?" asked Nampa in astonishment. "That's as bad as being a cannibal."

"If they poisoned you, then I believe that they are, indeed, cannibals," said one of the women.

"If they do not have any fire sticks," said Kimo, "then we can kill them easily."

"I still think we should move our village," said Gikita. "They would not find us in the jungle. Soon they would grow tired and give up. But if we kill them, other *cowodi* will hear. They will be angry and will not give up so easily. They will send out many woodbees to look for us. Sooner or later, they would find us."

"No, no," said Kimo. "If we kill them, that's the end of it."

"It has happened before," warned Gikita.

Niwa didn't know what to think. He didn't like his Aunt Mintaka, but he still hoped that she had not been eaten by the *cowodi*. It was hard for him to believe that they were cannibals. But it was obvious that most of the villagers now believed that the *cowodi* were cannibals and had probably eaten Mintaka and Dayuma, as well.

Everyone was getting very angry. The men were sharpening their spears and putting fresh poison on the darts for their blowguns. Talking excitedly, they made plans to go immediately to wipe out these white foreigners before the village was attacked. After all, they reasoned, what other excuse did the *cowodi* have for being in their jungle?

Then Mintaka walked boldly into the village.

Everyone gathered around her. "You escaped!" they said in amazement. "The *cowodi*'s poison must not be as strong as ours if it did not kill you."

At first Mintaka had no idea what made her such an attraction. She enjoyed the attention and smiled at everyone as they touched her.

Niwa pushed forward and asked, "Did they attack you?" But Mintaka ignored him; she was enjoying being the center of attention.

"But did the *cowodi* attack you?" demanded Niwa in a loud voice. "Did they try to eat you?"

Mintaka turned and frowned at him. "Of course they did not attack me," she said indignantly. "Whatever gave you such a foolish idea?"

"It's the poison," said Nankiwi, seeing that his lie was about to be exposed. "The poison has made her mind sick. She cannot remember."

"What are you talking about?" said Mintaka. "You are the one who is talking crazy."

With everyone talking at once, Nankiwi's story about being poisoned and attacked by the *cowodi* came spilling out.

"He is lying," Mintaka declared. "The *cowodi* did not attack us. I do not know whether they eat people sometimes or not, but they did not attack us. They were very friendly. They even took

Nankiwi for a ride in their woodbee."

The mention of Nankiwi's ride in the woodbee caused everyone to pause, because they had seen him in the sky.

"It was all part of a trick to get us to let down our guard," Nankiwi insisted. "But we saw through their trick and got away."

"Whether it was a trick or not," said Gikita, "the *cowodi* have always attacked us. If we do not kill them, then we must flee into the jungle. If we do not, I'm sure they will kill us sooner or later. It has always been so. We must choose—kill or flee."

Again everyone exploded into talking all at once. Late into the night around the fires the arguments continued. Exhausted, Niwa finally fell asleep in his hammock, not knowing what would happen the next day.

# Chapter 10

## Angels in the Sky

I T WAS MUCH LATER THAN USUAL when Niwa woke up the next morning. Fleeing from Nankiwi and sleeping out in the jungle had made him particularly tired. As he wandered out into the clearing, Niwa realized that several of the men of the village were gone. Had they gone to kill the *cowodi*? Nimonga, Dyuwi, Gikita, Kimo, Mincaye, and his older brother, Nampa, were nowhere to be seen. Kimo's wife, Dawa, seemed to be away, also. And Niwa noted that his mother and Aunt Mintaka were gone. Where Mintaka was, Niwa had no idea but figured that his mother was probably upstream making clay pots.

At least Nankiwi was still in the village . . . talking with Gimari, of course. Surely if the others had gone off to kill the *cowodi,* Nankiwi would have gone with them. After all, he was the one who had claimed that the *cowodi* were bad and had attacked them first. Relieved at seeing him, Niwa concluded that the villagers had abandoned the idea of killing the white men with the morning's light. *The men must have gone hunting,* Niwa thought.

There was a large catfish smoking over the coals of the fire. Niwa broke off a piece of it and began eating, spitting the bones into the fire. When he was finished, he licked his fingers and teased his pet monkey. He wanted to ask Gimari what the village adults had decided to do about the *cowodi,* but he hesitated to bring the subject up again with Nankiwi around. It might remind Nankiwi of their time in the jungle, so he simply said, "Gimari, where's mother?" He would go ask Akawo. She would certainly know what the group had decided about the *cowodi.*

Gimari responded as casually as if their mother had gone to harvest bananas. "Knowing it was right, she and Mintaka and Dawa went with the men to kill the *cowodi,*" she said.

"*What?*"

"Do your ears have no holes? You heard me," said Gimari. She and Nankiwi eyed Niwa as he considered this startling news.

Niwa was troubled. Why would his mother and

Mintaka go to kill the *cowodi*? His mother believed that Dayuma was living safely with the *cowodi*. And Mintaka had testified that the *cowodi* were not bad, that they had *not* attacked. It made no sense, and Niwa did not like the evil grin spreading over Nankiwi's face. Maybe Gimari was not telling the truth. Niwa got up and went to find Dabu and Moipa. Maybe they would know what was happening.

He found his friends upriver at the clay bank. They were engaged in one of their favorite pastimes— sliding down into the river. "Do you know where my mother and the men went?"

Moipa stood up in the river, water streaming down his face. "They went to kill the *cowodi*," he said. "We wanted to go, too, but they wouldn't let us."

"Are you sure? When did they go?"

"They left right after sunup," said Dabu.

Niwa looked up at the sky, and then his shoulders drooped. "Even running, I'll never catch them," he moaned. "They'd be almost to the Curaray River by now."

In shock, Niwa splashed across the river and took off down the trail into the jungle. He couldn't let the killing happen. He was sure that the woodbee had brought only good to his village. He would go and sound the alarm. Even if he ran, the war party would get there first. But maybe . . . maybe they would not attack right away. Often his people were very sly when planning to kill someone, looking for just the right time and place.

Niwa ran and ran until he thought his lungs

would burst. Then he half walked, half trotted until he caught his breath. Then he ran some more. Finally, as he came down the hill to where the river ran, he heard shouting and then some loud bangs, louder than he had ever heard before. Could that be the *cowodi*'s fire sticks Gikita had talked about? Had the attack already begun?

As Niwa came out of the jungle onto the beach, the first thing he saw was the bodies of the five *cowodi* floating in the river or crumpled on the beach with spears poking out of them. He had arrived too late! How could that be? He had tried so hard, run so long, but there was no question—the massacre had happened. He wanted to go look at the dead men, maybe to see if at least one was still breathing, but shock kept him rooted to his place at the edge of the jungle.

A tightening pain gripped his stomach and then cramped again until he lost what was left of the smoked catfish that he had eaten hours before. The bitterness in his mouth seemed right for such a bitter day.

What would happen now?

As he stood there, he became aware that the other Aucas were not staring in horror at their gruesome deed like he was. Instead, they were running around in confusion, pointing up into the air. Slowly, Niwa looked up, too, and gave a startled cry. The air above the river and the trees seemed to be filled with bright, dazzling beings, almost as if they were on fire. Was his mind playing tricks on him? Was the

sun too bright, giving him heatstroke? But the other
Aucas seemed to see them, too, pointing and crying

out in fear and astonishment.

Were these *cowodi* spirits—sent to avenge the men his people had come to kill? But for some strange reason, Niwa didn't feel afraid. The bright creatures had no weapons. And they weren't like any human beings he had ever seen before. They were clearly visible for anyone to see, but it was as though these strange creatures were made of shimmering water— something one could see but also see through.

Then Niwa was aware of a strange sound. It seemed to be coming from these bright beings in the air. He listened closely. The sound was like singing. It was very different than the one-note sounds his people made, but it *was* singing, nonetheless. Niwa looked this way and that. The sky seemed to be full of these brilliant creatures, like fireflies on a warm evening, but they were much larger and brighter, and their light didn't blink. The sound of their singing filled the whole canyon of the Curaray River. And then . . . slowly the vision faded—both the shimmering creatures and the sound of singing—until the sky was the dull blue of a normal jungle afternoon.

With the departure of the heavenly singing, fear seemed to settle over the small group of Aucas like a cold, damp fog. Niwa watched as they halfheartedly continued their vicious business by throwing the belongings of the *cowodi* into the river and destroying the woodbee. They tore its yellow skin off and left its bones lying on the beach.

When they were at the height of their destructive

activity, Niwa sneaked onto the beach and picked up a strip of the woodbee's yellow skin. It was tough and dry. He rolled it up like a snake skin and carried it with him as he disappeared back into the edge of the dense jungle.

In a short time, the other Aucas finished wrecking the *cowodi*'s camp and headed for home in silence.

Niwa followed along at the end of the line of subdued warriors. This was very different from battles they had won against other Aucas. His brother, Nampa, was holding his head with one hand, and Niwa could see that he staggered sometimes as he walked. When Nampa turned his head to the side, Niwa could see that he had been wounded. Blood was running down his cheek.

Back at Tiwaeno, the other villagers eagerly gathered around the war party and peppered them with questions.

"Did they use their fire sticks?"

"Yes," said Gikita. "Look at Nampa. He was hit on the side of his head, but it did not do much damage."

"It gave me a big headache," said Nampa. He sat on a log with his elbows on his knees and his head in both hands. "But the *cowodi* was not trying to kill me. It was just a small fire stick that he held in one hand."

"What makes you think he was not trying to kill you?" demanded his sister Gimari.

"Because," said Nampa, looking up at her, "until Mother grabbed his arm, he was just shooting up into the air—*bang, bang, bang*. Only when she pulled his arm down did the next bang hit me. It knocked me to the ground, but when I looked at him, he was just as surprised as I was. He was not trying to kill me. I'm sure of it."

"Dawa was hit, too," said Mintaka. "But the fire stick did not hurt her much."

Dawa stood up so everyone could see her wounds. She pointed to a very small wound on her wrist and another above her knee. "They do not hurt much," she said.

Nankiwi spoke up. "The *cowodi* must not be as powerful as you say, Gikita, if this is all the damage their noisy fire sticks can do."

"You are wrong, you coward! You would not even come with us. They were not trying to kill us. Ask Dawa. She and the other women were across the river hidden in the trees. The one with the long fire stick did not even know she was there. It was only an accident that she was hit. And you heard Nampa. The *cowodi* was not trying to kill him."

"Then what were they trying to do?" challenged Nankiwi.

Gikita shrugged. "Maybe they were trying to scare us with the big bang."

Kimo then spoke up. "One of them kept saying, 'Why are you killing us? We just want to meet you.'"

"What does that mean?" challenged Nankiwi. "You are brave warriors. You had defeated them. What else could they do but beg for mercy?"

"We had not yet defeated them at that point," said Kimo. "They could have shot us, but they didn't."

Then Niwa's mother spoke up. "That same man could have run away," said Akawo. "He was in the middle of the river, and no one was near him. Instead, he just stood there until Kimo came out to him and speared him. He was no coward."

"That's right," said Kimo. "They were very brave. Besides, they had many, many spirit warriors in the sky who could have easily destroyed us."

This was the first mention of the shining beings Niwa had seen, and the boy was eager to see if the others saw what he had seen.

"Warrior spirits in the sky?" scoffed Nankiwi. "Whoever heard of such a thing? You must have been the one hit on the head like Nampa."

"I was *not* hit on the head," insisted Kimo. "Ask anyone else what they saw, and they'll tell you the same."

"I saw them," said Gikita. "They were bright, shiny creatures who flew in the sky above the *cowodi*. You should have heard the beautiful sounds they made."

Several other of the warriors agreed. "We expected them to attack us, but they didn't," they said.

Then Gimari spoke up. "Maybe they were more woodbees. Woodbees fly in the sky and make noise."

Niwa couldn't keep quiet any longer. "No," he

104

said. "Woodbees make a lot of noise, but they don't sing. These spirits were singing beautiful sounds. And you could see through them—like clear river water."

Nankiwi scowled at Niwa as though responding to someone so young was unnecessary and beneath him.

"The thing I still don't understand," said Gikita slowly, "is why didn't they defend themselves? There must be some reason. Why would the *cowodi* let themselves be killed rather than kill us? This I do not understand!"

Again the arguments went on around the village fires late into the night, but no one seemed to have a good answer for Gikita's question.

# Chapter 11

# Chaos

THE NEXT DAY, three woodbees flew over Tiwaeno. They were not yellow like the one the Aucas wrecked along the Curaray River. One was silver, and two were dark green. They flew low over the village and circled many times, but they did not lower any gifts to the people.

"This is not good," said Gikita. "Being very angry, the *cowodi* are coming to kill us. We should not have attacked them. Now we will have to leave our village."

"I thought we killed them so that they *wouldn't* bother us anymore," snapped Mintaka. "Now you are telling us that they are coming again."

"Yes," said Gikita. "Knowing what happened in the past, we should not have killed. Years ago, we killed just one *cowodi* and for months others chased us through the jungle with their fire sticks. Now we have killed five. Certainly great revenge will be taken against us."

This time the villagers listened to him. That evening, Kimo and Dawa gathered up their few possessions and headed off into the jungle with their three small children trailing along behind them. "We are going to join some other Auca village," said Kimo. "We cannot live here any longer."

It was not unheard of for Aucas to move to another village, even to one with which they had been at war. An "outsider" was usually tolerated—if not welcomed—until he or she was recognized as a member of the new village. This process could take from a few months to a year. If the person was never accepted as a member, he or she usually moved on or returned to their original village.

*But to leave at night,* thought Niwa as he watched Kimo and Dawa and their children walk into the jungle, *they must be more frightened of the* cowodi *than of the anaconda or the jaguar.*

The next day another woodbee flew over their village. It was a very different-looking one. It had no wings, and no one had ever seen anything like it. It looked like a mosquito with one huge bubble-shaped eye in the front. It hung over the village and hummed very loudly.

All of the Aucas—even Niwa and his mother—

ran off into the tropical jungle.

"Oh no," wailed Akawo, tears streaming down her cheeks. "What have we done? Being right, Gikita warned us that the *cowodi* would come to take revenge." And then she gave another great cry as though she were facing a new tragedy. "And if Dayuma has been living with the *cowodi*, she will certainly be killed now."

"Maybe not, Mother," comforted Niwa. "Even though three woodbees flew over yesterday, the *cowodi* did not attack us. Maybe Dayuma has spoken for us and asked them not to kill us."

"Being only an Auca, what power could she have?" asked his mother. "We know that the *cowodi* have killed many of our people in the past." She turned to her older son. "What do you think, Nampa? You fought with them. Could Dayuma speak for us?"

Nampa, whose head still hurt so badly that he could barely walk, muttered, "I do not know. I do not care," and staggered on.

Niwa and his mother stopped and waited beside a small stream while Nampa continued on down the jungle trail. The boy and his mother waited a long time, long after the noise of the mosquito-woodbee had gone away. Then they carefully returned to the village.

Other people had returned as well and were preparing to move. Arguments erupted over various possessions, especially the gifts the woodbee had dropped to the people. One person wanted an ax, another claimed a machete, someone else grabbed one of the cooking pots. The only gifts the people did not fight over were the clothes. Most people tore them off and threw them into the fire. They did not want to look like the *cowodi*. They did not really want to have the things that would connect them to the *cowodi*, but the pots and machetes and axes were far too valuable to discard.

Niwa, however, did not throw away his piece of woodbee skin. Instead, he had wrapped it around his blowgun and tied it with a piece of vine.

Niwa had not seen Nankiwi or Gimari all day and assumed that they had already run off, but Nankiwi's other wife was herding the children down to the river. Each child carried his or her hammock and a few other items as they splashed across the shallows and disappeared into the jungle on the other side.

"Mother," said Niwa, "are we going to leave, too? Almost everyone else has gone."

Akawo sat in her hammock, staring into the ashes of their dead cooking fire. She had been sitting there all morning. It was unusual for her to let the fire go out. Now they would have to find a coal from someone else's fire with which to light theirs.

"Mother," persisted Niwa, very worried by how listless Akawo appeared, "feeling hungry, I'm going to go spear some fish. Why don't you get the fire going, and we'll eat when I come back."

Niwa hiked down the river with his spear. He knew where a big log lay in the water. Fish often gathered in the pool on the other side. But he was worried about his mother. He had never seen her like this. It was as though all the fight and all the hope had gone out of her. But then, that was the way he felt, too. What was left for them? Their village was breaking up. The *cowodi* seemed to be after them, people were leaving in fear, and now his mother . . . she seemed to be fading away into a dream world.

But when Niwa returned home with two catfish, he found that Akawo had more than "faded away"; she had disappeared. In fact, the only other person who was in the village was Aunt Mintaka. She was going from house to house, rummaging through everything that had been left behind, taking things she thought were valuable when she found them.

"Where's my mother?" demanded Niwa.

"Who can hear her?" Mintaka shrugged. "Everyone's gone into the jungle. How can I see your mother if she is away?" She picked up a small clay pot and looked it over carefully, then dropped it into her sack of possessions.

For fear that Mintaka would take them, Niwa did not leave the catfish at his house, where there was still no fire in the fireplace. Instead, he took them with him as he went upriver to the clay bank. Maybe his mother was making clay pots. She often went there to dig her hands into the soft, reddish brown clay when she was upset. Working with it seemed to calm her.

But she was not there!

He called for her and searched a short distance

into the jungle along each of the trails that led from the village. Still, he could not find her. Now Niwa was really worried. A heavy feeling sat in the pit of his stomach.

When he returned to Tiwaeno, even Mintaka had gone. Niwa wandered around feeling alone and frightened. Heavy clouds had gathered and covered the sky. It would rain soon. He wished he still had his pet parrot to keep him company, but he had given the parrot to the *cowodi*. Briefly he wondered whether they kept him as a pet or ate him.

Evening was approaching, and the empty village was cloaked in an unreal bluish light. In his own house, Niwa sat on his hammock and looked around. His mother's hammock was still there, as were her clay cooking pots. A bunch of bananas hung from the roof, nearly ripe. Her sack of woven palm strands hung on the stub of a branch on one of the support poles. It did not look like she had gone away for good.

*On the other hand,* thought Niwa, *in her dazed condition, Mother may have wandered off into the jungle without taking anything with her.* What was he to do? If he went out searching for her, she might come back and not find him. Then she might think he had left. But if he stayed . . . she might need help.

The first drops of rain splattering hard on the ground outside his house brought him out of his thoughts. This was going to be a heavy storm. He wished his mother were here and not out in the jungle, but there was no hope of finding her in the middle of a violent tropical storm.

Then he remembered: His fire was out, and he had no way of making a new one. He raced outside and went from house to house. Finally, in Gikita's house he found some smoldering coals beneath the ashes. He scooped them up in a clay pot and ran for home. There, by blowing them to life and adding some dry fuel, he soon had a fire.

*At least if my mother comes home, I will have a warm fire to help her dry off,* he thought. Then he arranged the catfish on sticks over the blaze and lay back on his hammock, waiting for them to cook as the rain poured down outside.

The next morning, Niwa was still alone in the empty village. He decided that he had to search for Akawo. In the condition he had last seen her, his mother wouldn't be able to take care of herself. She could be hurt or sick or lost. He had to find her.

Niwa gathered up his spear, blowgun, and darts and wrapped some burning coals in a palm leaf and put them in a small clay pot so that he would have fire. Then he went off looking for his mother.

For five days, Niwa searched the jungle. Finally he found her nearly dead, curled up between the roots of a pepper kapok tree. He brought her water from one of the mountain streams and found bananas and other jungle fruit for her to eat. After building a simple shelter of bamboo and palm fronds, and leaving a burning fire, he left her for short periods to go fishing and hunting. As the weeks passed, Akawo's strength began to return, and Niwa became a good hunter.

The boy and his mother lived alone in the jungle for months, wandering from place to place in search of food, making lean-to huts of palm branches to keep off the heavy rain, but never building a proper house or joining permanently with another village.

Sometimes they visited other Auca villages and stayed for a week or two, but sooner or later, Akawo got restless and fearful and headed off into the jungle again. Niwa had to go after her.

One day they found Niwa's sister Gimari and Ipa, one of Nankiwi's other wives, living in one of the villages. They said that Ipa's brother had speared Nankiwi when they got into a fight. "So now," shrugged Gimari, "being alone, we live together."

From Gimari they also learned that their brother Nampa had died on a hunting trip, but the story was not clear how he had died. Some said his head started hurting again so badly that he just died on the trail. Others said that an anaconda had crushed him to death.

But in spite of finding Gimari, who had had a child before Nankiwi died, Niwa could not persuade his mother to stay in that village and rebuild their family. "No," Akawo said, "having a baby, she has her own life now. By myself, I must find Dayuma." It was the first time since leaving Tiwaeno that she had mentioned Dayuma, but suddenly Niwa realized what made his mother so restless. In her confused mind, she was still looking for Dayuma. Unless his oldest sister was still alive and they somehow miraculously found her, they might never settle down. But how could they find her wandering around in the jungle? If she were alive at all, she was with the *cowodi*. It seemed like a hopeless situation.

Niwa and Akawo continued to drift from place to

place for over two years until one day, when the fruit of the kapok tree was ripe, they arrived at the village that Gikita had adopted as his new home. To their great surprise, Aunt Mintaka and Gikita's wife, Mankamu, had also just arrived. They had a most remarkable story.

One year earlier, the two women had fled the jungle and had been taken in by some friendly *cowodi.* "No, no," they assured everyone, "the *cowodi* are not cannibals and did not hurt us. Furthermore," they said triumphantly, "we found Dayuma! Dayuma is alive and well!"

The first smile Niwa had seen in many months spread over his mother's face.

As Akawo had suspected, her daughter had been living with the *cowodi* all these years and could speak their language. And together Dayuma, Mintaka, and Mankamu had taught some of the *cowodi* their own language. "But the *cowodi* have very bad ears," sniffed Mintaka. "They could not understand much."

Then the women said something even more surprising. Dayuma wanted to come home and bring two *cowodi* women to live with the Aucas.

"So," said Mankamu to her husband, Gikita, "having heard all that we've told you, will you move back to Tiwaeno and build a new house? Will you ask all the old families to come back?"

Gikita sat for a long time, looking back and forth at the two women who had been away living with the *cowodi.* Finally, he said in a soft voice, "Seeing that you have not been eaten, I believe that the *cowodi* are not cannibals and that we killed them for no good reason. I will go back."

Chapter 12

# Reunion

GIKITA'S WILLINGNESS TO RETURN to Tiwaeno excited Akawo, and the prospect of seeing her daughter Dayuma again changed her whole mood. Suddenly she had something for which to live.

This made Niwa joyful, too. His mother no longer walked around as though she were in a daze. He didn't have to worry whether he would wake up the next morning to find that she had wandered off into the jungle during the night. Niwa and his mother had plans to make. They had things to do. They also would return to Tiwaeno, and life would be different. For the first time in two years they had hope.

But first they had a journey

to make. In their travels they had discovered where all the Tiwaeno families had fled, so it was their task to visit those villages again and convince the refugees to return.

It took three weeks to visit all the former members of Tiwaeno, and Niwa and Akawo were among the last to arrive back at their old village. They did not find everyone. Some, like Nankiwi, had died, leaving Gimari and his other wives as widows. But in other families new babies had been born, and there were a couple new marriages.

When Niwa and his mother walked into the clearing beside the Tiwaeno River, they could see that nothing was left of their old house. But everyone was glad to see them.

"You will live with us!" shouted Gimari and Ipa, Nankiwi's widows. Some of the men had helped them build a house. This in itself was unusual for the Aucas. Normally, no one helped their neighbor unless they got something out of it for themselves. The only truly cooperative efforts were hunting and fishing.

Akawo smiled at her daughter Gimari. It was a nice offer, especially since there had been so many bad feelings between them. But she appeared a little uncertain. Soon she said, "Who is that new house for—the one with the walls?" Niwa and Akawo had passed a new house on their way into the village. No hammocks were hung inside, but a couple of the men were busy putting up walls of split bamboo. This, too, was very unusual because

Auca houses seldom had walls.

"Oh, that's for the white women," said Gimari. "Mintaka and Mankamu say they must have walls. It's what they are used to."

Niwa looked around. "Where is Aunt Mintaka?" he asked.

"I do not see her," shrugged Gimari in the way so common to how the Aucas answered any question. "She and several others went to get the white women. Being away for many days, their return will be soon."

As the sun slipped below the trees in the late afternoon two days later, a whole line of people came down the trail, waded across the river, and entered the village. "They've come! They've come!" shouted the younger children. Excitedly, everyone left their hammocks and their fires and gathered around to see them.

In all the talk about *cowodi* and outsiders, Niwa had never really imagined what white people looked like. The men in the woodbee had been too far away to see well. Now he simply stared at the two white women standing in the clearing. Their hair was brown like the river after a hard rain, but their skin was not actually white; it just lacked color, like someone who was sick. *No, that's not quite right. They just have pale faces,* thought Niwa as he struggled to keep his place near the front of the little crowd that had gathered to stare at the two women and one . . . "Oh, my goodness," said Niwa aloud. "Look at her!"

There, riding on the back of a Quechua Indian, was a little girl not more than three years old. Her skin was as pale as that of the women, but her hair was as bright as the sun and fluffy like a cloud. Her eyes sparkled with the blue of a clear sky. Niwa couldn't believe what he was seeing. This alone was worth coming back to Tiwaeno. It was far more curious than seeing all the unusual birds of the jungle at the same time.

Suddenly, there was a loud cry, and someone came crashing through the crowd, knocking people aside to the right and left. It was his mother, Akawo. She ran past the white people and threw her arms around an Indian woman Niwa did not know.

"My Dayuma, my Dayuma," she cried over and over as tears streamed down her face, filling every careworn line. "Now arriving, you have come home."

Niwa pressed forward to get a better look at this stranger. Was she really his oldest sister? Niwa realized that he could not remember what she had looked like before she left. He had thought he remembered her, but it must have been a fantasy he had created to represent his lost sister.

This woman wore clothes like the white women, but her hair was cut in the Auca way and her earlobes hung in large loops, indicating that they had once been stretched by the balsa wood disks characteristic of his people. The more Niwa studied Dayuma's face, he could see that she had the family resemblance. He looked at Gimari. She was grinning shyly and inching forward, her baby on her hip. He wondered if she could remember clearly. He wished that his older brother, Nampa, were still alive. He would have remembered for sure.

That night there was a great feast—an unusual event for Aucas. Even the Quechua Indians who had come with the white women were welcomed to join in the festivities, though they seemed frightened and kept indicating that they wanted to go home. Niwa understood. Aucas had killed many Quechuas over the years, and seldom allowed them into their territory. But Dayuma—Niwa was getting used to the idea that she was his sister—kept assuring the Quechuas that they were safe and could leave the next day.

Dayuma had learned the language of the white people and introduced them at the feast. "This woman, who is so very tall, is Elisabeth Elliot. I call her *Gikari*."

*Gikari,* mused Niwa curiously. *Gikari* meant "woodpecker" in the Auca language. He wondered why that was her name.

Then Dayuma's face became very somber, and she swallowed several times as though she was having a hard time speaking the next words. Finally, in a pinched voice full of emotion, she said, "Loving her husband, whom you have killed, she has come to share God's love with you."

Everyone fell silent, so silent that the only thing that could be heard was the crackling of the fire and the hum of the night insects in the nearby jungle. The Aucas had a word for God. They believed that He had made all people. But the idea that He loved them was entirely new. It felt too big for Niwa's thinking. But something about it seemed very real, especially when he remembered the warrior spirits who had hovered over the dead white men at the Curaray River. God must have loved them.

Finally, Gikita coughed and said, "You are saying that this tall woman was married to one of the *cowodi* we killed on the Curaray River?"

"They were not *cowodi*. They were not cannibals. They may have been strangers, but they didn't eat people. They were good," corrected Dayuma.

Gikita nodded. "But is this one the wife of one of those men?"

"Yes," said Dayuma. "His name was Jim Elliot. The little girl, Valerie, is his daughter."

Turning to the second woman, Dayuma continued, "And this woman with her hair rolled back from her face is Rachel Saint. I call her *Nimu*."

*Nimu . . . star,* thought Niwa. *Now, that's a nice name.*

"She is the sister of the man who flew the yellow woodbee," Dayuma went on. "His name was Nate . . . Nate Saint." Dayuma stopped, and everyone remained silent. They knew that they had killed him, also, at the Curaray River. They had also killed the yellow woodbee so that it could not fly.

The Aucas, who up till now had found it difficult

to take their eyes off the curious white women, now looked down at the ground and studied their toes. Finally, Gikita said quietly, "In killing them, we did not do well. It was not necessary."

At this the white women smiled, the tension was broken, and the festivities went on late into the night.

The Aucas were not afraid of these white outsiders. Certainly two women and a little child had not been sent for revenge! But they still could not understand why the foreigners had come to live among them. The women would sit for long periods of time, making marks on white leaves. From time to time, the white women tried to explain what they were doing, but they could not speak well—Dayuma said that they should cut the hair in front of their ears so they could hear. After all, one had to hear well if one wanted to speak properly.

Niwa visited the women's house often. He liked to watch them. Everything they did seemed awkward or different. They wore clothes on their whole body— even their feet. They didn't squat by the fire to cook their food; instead they bent over or kneeled on the ground. Sometimes they pointed to something—a spear, a drinking gourd, a sudden rain, or two children arguing—and asked him, "What is the word for that?" And then they would make black scratchings on the white leaves.

Niwa asked questions, too. "Why do you scrub your teeth with that funny stick?" "What are you wearing on your feet?" and "Why do you make those scratches on the white leaves?"

One day, Nimu said something that finally made sense to Niwa. "We have come to work on 'God's Carving,' " she said.

"God's Carving?" said Niwa with a frown.

"Yes. God's words . . . ah . . ." she fumbled, "saved as a carving so you can know what He said."

"He has done this? He has spoken to us?"

"Yes. God loved the Aucas so much that He wanted you to know about Him and have His words in a carving so everyone could hear them."

The idea that God loved the Auca people was still knew to Niwa. He had never had anyone say that they loved him. He knew . . . at least he thought he knew that his mother loved him. But then she had to; she was his mother. But love was a rare thing in his village.

After that, Niwa came every day to talk to Gikari or Nimu. He liked it when the little girl, Valerie, came running to show him a feather or just held his hand in a friendly way. One day he brought his blowgun and carefully unwrapped the piece of yellow skin from the woodbee's wing that he had saved. He showed it to Gikari. "I wanted to stop the killing," he said with tears in his eyes. "But I was too late. Now believing that God loves me, I want to follow His ways. But . . . will He forgive me for not stopping the killing?"

"Yes, yes, He will forgive you," said Gikari. "We all had a hand in killing His Son because of our wrong ways, and He has forgiven us all."

These were strange and wonderful ideas. Revenge, not forgiveness, was the Auca way. If the Aucas learned to forgive—in the way that Gikari and Nimu seemed to forgive them for killing the five men—it might change the Auca way forever. Niwa wondered whether his people wanted to be changed. But then the old ways of killing and revenge and hatred had been destroying them. Weren't they always running? Weren't they always afraid? No one could grow old. *Without changing to God's way, we might disappear from the jungle forever,* he thought.

A strange happiness filled Niwa inside. If they listened to these women and followed God's ways, the Aucas might have a future after all.

## Chapter 13

# Return to Palm Beach

SATURDAY MORNING, the day before Easter, 1965, dawned bright and clear. It was nine years after the five missionaries had been killed by the Aucas, and fourteen-year-old Steve Saint woke to the demanding words of his pet parrot. "Gimme, gimme, gimme. Gimme a nut. Gimme a nut."

Steve sat up in his hammock, tied between poles in a strange Indian house and looked around, uncertain, for a moment, where he was. Then it came back to him. The evening before, he and his sister, Kathie, had landed at the small airstrip that had been hacked out of the jungle near the village of Tiwaeno in Ecuador. They had come with his aunt,

Rachel Saint, and another missionary to deliver the first copies of the Gospel of Mark, translated and printed in the Auca language.

"Gimme a nut. Gimme a nut," continued the parrot, and Steve groaned to himself. Sometimes he wondered why he took that demanding bird with him *everywhere* he went. But he knew the reason. It reminded him of his missionary-pilot father, Nate Saint.

Steve got up and went over to rummage through his duffel bag. Somewhere in there he had some peanuts for that crazy bird, but where? And then suddenly the parrot became quiet. Steve glanced back over his shoulder and saw a young Auca man standing there. He was grinning the biggest grin Steve had ever seen and was feeding the parrot a banana.

Steve got up, nodded, and said, "Hi."

The Auca responded awkwardly with, "Hi." Then he started pointing back and forth to himself and then the parrot, saying, "Bird . . . my. Bird . . . my." He made a lot of other gestures with his hands, ending by locking his thumbs together with his hands outstretched and swooping them around in the air as though they were an airplane.

Steve called his Aunt Rachel over and said, "He's saying, 'Bird, my,' and making a bunch of signs in the air. What does he mean?"

After a few moments of conversation in Auca, Rachel Saint introduced Steve to Niwa and explained that the parrot had belonged to Niwa when he was a boy. He had been the one who had put it in a cage and sent it to the white people. Niwa was so excited to see it again that he couldn't help but try to thank Steve for bringing it to visit.

The tall, lanky, blond-haired Steve shook hands with the strong, young Auca man, and they both did more gestures, trying to communicate that the parrot had belonged to both of them.

"Tomorrow will be a great day for Niwa," explained Rachel after a few moments. "He has been a believer for a long time, but on Easter he will be baptized. We are all going to the Curaray River to celebrate God's Carving and have a baptism. I didn't know about the baptism until we arrived last night. I hope that's okay with you."

Steve frowned. This was more than he had expected.

"I'm sorry," said his aunt. "I thought we were going to have the celebration here—just for God's Carving. But Pastor Kimo has planned everything, and it includes the baptism."

Steve gulped. The Curaray River . . . that was where his father had been killed. He wasn't sure he wanted to go there—not yet, at least. It was enough to come and visit this village where the men who had killed his father still lived. He knew that his Aunt Rachel and Elisabeth Elliot had shared the Gospel with them, and many had become believers, and on one level, he had forgiven them. But to visit his father's grave? That might be too much.

After his father and the others had been killed,

Ecuadorian soldiers and missionary representatives who searched for the five men found the bodies in the river beside the wrecked airplane. After consulting with the men's wives by radio, they decided that the men would be buried there, under the tree house at Palm Beach. But Steve had never visited the grave. Someday he wanted to ... but not with the same men who had killed his dad.

Elisabeth Elliot and her little daughter, Valerie, had spent two years living with the Aucas, telling them about Jesus. Rachel Saint had stayed on and, with the help of Dayuma, had learned the Aucas' language, reduced it to writing, taught the people how to read, and then began translating the New Testament. Now there was not only a thriving church in Tiwaeno, but the people were eager to get their own copies of "God's Carving" to read themselves.

One of the first Aucas to have become a Christian was Kimo, and he was now the pastor of the Auca church.

As the villagers and guests walked through the jungle toward the Curaray River on Easter Sunday morning, Steve and his sister, Kathie, walked along with them. Steve not only had made up his mind to make the journey, but he had come to another decision.

He had already decided to follow Jesus, but he hadn't yet been baptized. However, as he thought about how these once-savage people, who had been killing themselves off with their constant warfare and cruelty, had been rescued from the brink of extinction by the Gospel, he felt a new appreciation for God's love.

He had walked around the village, noting the families and little house used for a church and a school. He heard children singing and knew they no longer lived in fear of attack. He met Gikita, now older than any Auca could ever remember a man living, even though he was only fifty. There was peace in the village.

All of this helped Steve understand as he had never understood before why his father had risked his life to bring them the Gospel. With that understanding came a deeper forgiveness for those who had killed the man he idolized and the other missionaries.

Not only would he make the hike to Palm Beach, he and Kathie had asked to be baptized there.

Palm Beach ... just a simple sandbar along the Curaray River in the jungles of Ecuador. Solemnly the procession came out of the shady jungle into the Easter sunshine along the banks of the shallow river. And on that Easter Sunday morning, five people were baptized at Palm Beach. Three were Aucas: Niwa and two young people—Oncaye and Iniwa. And two were the children of Nate Saint—Steve and Kathie.

Pastor Kimo, one of the men who had helped kill the missionaries on that very spot nine years before, led the baptismal service. Afterward, Kimo looked over at the graves of the missionaries under the tall ironwood tree and prayed, "Lord, long ago, not knowing You, we sinned right here. Now, believing in You, we are going to meet You in the air!"

# More About the Ecuador Martyrs

THE NAME *AUCA* is a term of contempt meaning savage. It was given to these reclusive Indians by their Quechuan neighbors. At the time, it was an apt name in every sense; their killing extended not only to any outsider but plagued their tribal life with unending feuds and wanton killing at every level, even to the practice of burying a living child with its dead parent.

These people enjoyed no organized sports, festivals, or religion (other than a general fear of the jungle spirits). There was no civic law or respect for elders or leaders; raw power controlled everything. There was no neighborly cooperation or organization (except in the hunt). Though they observed many taboos, they had no written language and only a limited oral history or tradition.

Indeed, they were so savage and so lacking in the social restraints commonly known as "civilization" that they were a dying people, whether or not the outside world overwhelmed them in its search for oil.

But they called themselves Waorani (sometimes written, *Huaorani*) meaning, "the people," and God loved them enough to reach out to them through His servants, who became known as the five Ecuador martyrs.

The story of the five missionaries who were killed in the jungles of Ecuador on Sunday, January 8, 1956, may have inspired more young people to dedicate their lives to Christian service in the last half of the twentieth century than any other event.

This was partially because of the prompt media attention their deaths received. (One radio operator at the North Pole overheard Nate Saint's radio call to his wife on January 7 to say that they had made contact with the Aucas. The man at the North Pole listened in again the next day at the appointed time only to realize that there was no response from Nate.) Thirteen years earlier five New Tribes missionaries were killed in the jungles of Bolivia. Without radio contact and close support by airplane, their fate was uncertain for three agonizing years. But with Operation Auca in Ecuador, possibly for the first time, Christian martyrdom was announced to the world within hours of the event. Radio communications mobilized mission and government officials to organize a search party the following day. A *Time* magazine correspondent and a *Life* magazine photographer were dispatched to the scene while the world breathlessly waited for more news.

But more significant was the public revelation of the character of these missionaries. Not that others were less dedicated, but the news was so fresh that these five men seemed like peers, the guys next door. Quotes from Jim Elliot's personal journal, for instance, gripped Christians everywhere when he wrote, "He is no fool who gives what he cannot keep to gain what he cannot lose," or "I seek not a long life but a full one, like you, Lord Jesus."

Three of the men were recent graduates of Wheaton College: Nate Saint, Jim Elliot, and Ed McCully, who had been a star football player at the Midwestern Christian college. Roger Youderian had been a World War II paratrooper and a graduate of Northwestern College in Minneapolis. Pete Fleming had excelled as an athlete and student, ultimately getting his masters degree from the University of Washington. These were guys with whom everyone could identify. And their sacrifice left behind five widows and nine fatherless children. It was natural for Christian young people to wonder, "It could have been me. . . . Maybe *I* should volunteer!"

In Christian schools and colleges around the world, hundreds of young people dedicated their lives to missionary service to replace the fallen five. Others who peg the beginning of their Christian ministry to the impact of the "Auca martyrs" include pastor and writer Charles Swindoll, speaker and author Josh

McDowell, and Don Stephens, president of Youth With A Mission's Mercy Ships.

But perhaps the most stirring "relay runners" to pick up the torch were Elisabeth Elliot and Rachel Saint—wife and sister of two of the fallen men—who returned to the tribe a little over two years after the massacre. Elisabeth even took her three-year-old daughter, Valerie, and stayed a little over two years. Rachel lived with the tribe for thirty-four years until her failing health required her departure. Their courage profoundly influenced the Indians.

The Aucas remembered and often spoke among themselves of the *cowodi* who had come in the yellow "woodbee." Two things perplexed them: Why hadn't the white men used their guns to defend themselves? And what caused the singing and bright lights that had floated above the trees after their deaths (a phenomena confirmed by all the living eyewitness and reported in print by Olive Fleming in 1990 and Steve Saint in 1996)? The Aucas' conclusion was that the missionaries had been peaceful and good, and their deaths had stirred a profound spiritual event.

These assumptions opened them to the Gospel that Elisabeth Elliot and Rachel Saint shared, and in time, almost the entire tribe became Christians.

Sometimes critics accuse missionaries of destroying native cultures, and all too often western ideas have been substituted where the Gospel did not require any change. But the conversion of the Aucas to Christianity probably saved them from physical extinction. Not only were they killing themselves off with their constant murders and tribal wars, but their primitive hostility made them targets for the ruthless raiders of the jungle's treasures—whether it was gold, rubber, oil, wood, or land.

However, since accepting Christ and learning to read, their life has changed dramatically for the better. The family life which once lacked fathers and uncles for many of the children now commonly includes grandparents, even great-grandparents. One example is Gikita, who at the time of the massacre was the oldest man in his village at about age forty. There were only seven adult men in the village then—such was the result of all the killings. However, with the peace brought by the Gospel, Gikita lived to the age of eighty, not dying until February 11, 1997.

Living out the Gospel became quite literal for Nate Saint and the other martyrs. Like Jesus, they gave their lives that others might live—both spiritually and physically.

## For Further Reading

Elliot, Elisabeth. *The Savage My Kinsman*. New York: Harper and Brothers, 1961.
Elliot, Elisabeth. *Through Gates of Splendor*. New York: Harper and Brothers, 1957.
Hitt, Russell T. *Jungle Pilot: The Life and Witness of Nate Saint*. Grand Rapids, Mich.: Zondervan, 1973.

Kingsland, Rosemary. *A Saint Among Savages*. London: Collins, 1980.

Liefield, Olive Fleming. *Unfolding Destinies*. Grand Rapids, Mich.: Zondervan, 1990.

Saint, Steve. "Did They Have to Die?" in *Christianity Today*, September 16, 1996, pp. 20-27.

*Tell Them We Are Not Auca; We Are Waorani,* a 28 min. video featuring Gikita telling his life story. He is interviewed by James Yost, a Summer Institute of Linguistics anthropologist. It is available through International Academic Bookstore, Box C94, 7500 W. Camp Wisdom Rd., Dallas, TX 75236-5628.

Wallis, Ethel Emily. *Aucas Downriver*. New York: Harper and Row, 1973.

Wallis, Ethel Emily. *The Dayuma Story*. New York: Harper and Row, 1960.

White, Kathleen. *Jim Elliot*. Minneapolis, Minn.: Bethany House, 1990.

# Series for Middle Graders*
## From Bethany House Publishers

**ADVENTURES DOWN UNDER • by Robert Elmer**
When Patrick McWaid's father is unjustly sent to Australia as a prisoner in 1867, the rest of the family follows, uncovering action-packed mystery along the way.

**ADVENTURES OF THE NORTHWOODS • by Lois Walfrid Johnson**
Kate O'Connell and her stepbrother Anders encounter mystery and adventure in northwest Wisconsin near the turn of the century.

**AN AMERICAN ADVENTURE SERIES • by Lee Roddy**
Hildy Corrigan and her family must overcome danger and hardship during the Great Depression as they search for a "forever home."

**BLOODHOUNDS, INC. • by Bill Myers**
Hilarious, hair-raising suspense follows brother-and-sister detectives Sean and Melissa Hunter in these madcap mysteries with a message.

**JOURNEYS TO FAYRAH • by Bill Myers**
Join Denise, Nathan, and Josh on amazing journeys as they discover the wonders and lessons of the mystical Kingdom of Fayrah.

**MANDIE BOOKS • by Lois Gladys Leppard**
With over four million sold, the turn-of-the-century adventures of Mandie and her many friends will keep readers eager for more.

**THE RIVERBOAT ADVENTURES • by Lois Walfrid Johnson**
Libby Norstad and her friend Caleb face the challenges and risks of working with the Underground Railroad during the mid–1800s.

**TRAILBLAZER BOOKS • by Dave and Neta Jackson**
Follow the exciting lives of real-life Christian heroes through the eyes of child characters as they share their faith and God's love with others around the world.

**THE TWELVE CANDLES CLUB • by Elaine L. Schulte**
When four twelve-year-old girls set up a business doing odd jobs and baby-sitting, they find themselves in the midst of wacky adventures and hilarious surprises.

**THE YOUNG UNDERGROUND • by Robert Elmer**
Peter and Elise Andersen's plots to protect their friends and themselves from Nazi soldiers in World War II Denmark guarantee fast-paced action and suspenseful reads.

*(ages 8–13)